PRAISE FOR BRANDON APPLEGATE

"Those We Left Behind is a heaping dish of diverse horror stories with a side of human tenderloin served rare. Applegate delivers the goods and then some."

— Joshua Marsella, author of *Scratches* and *Hunger For Death*

Those We Left Behind offers eerie tension and creepy visuals that make the reader look out the window, into the woods, and even down the drain with a little more caution. Each story hooks into the heart, dragging the reader, bloodied and broken, through fantastical darkness. And when you think you've had enough, Applegate peels open your eyes to face the darkness in your soul.

— Red Lagoe, author of *Lucid Screams* and *Dismal Dreams*

"In Applegate's stunning debut, family horrors get a fresh coat of the blackest, bleakest paint, but a deep compassion shines through the darkness. These stories will make your heart race and ache in equal measure."

— Eric Raglin, author of *Nightmare Yearnings*

"Brandon Applegate knows what drives horror. In *Those We Left Behind and Other Sacrifices*, Applegate expertly mines the terrors found in love's fears and failures, but he also finds the fragile magic that binds us together despite the darkness. The gory, the gross, the gripping, the ghostly, the grand - Applegate unearths the beating, haunted heart of the genre again and again."

— Gordon B. White, author of *Rookfield*

"I can't say enough good things about this collection of short stories. Those We Left Behind and Other Sacrifices may be Applegate's debut collection, but only in name. He delivers a wide-ranging suite of stories with the skill of a veteran wordsmith. There's creeping dread, shocking twists, gruesome gore, and even a little bit of magic...but what stood out most to me was the heart beating within these stories. I could tell in the first few stories alone that one of Applegate's strengths is pouring a foundation of raw emotion for each tale and letting it fortify every setting and each character. These stories aren't hollow horror, oh no; these babies have soul. But, beware, for the heart pumping blood throughout this book is blackened, battered, and bruised, and is quick to torment."

— Alex Ebenstein, editor-in-chief of Dread Stone Press

"In *Those We Left Behind*, Brandon Applegate crafts fully-realized worlds of horror and despair through the medium of short fiction. He builds worlds that ensnare readers, letting them go only when he's struck the perfect notes of fear."

— Patrick Barb, horror author featured in *Humans are the Problem*, *Tales to Terrify*, and *Boneyard Soup Magazine*

"Brandon Applegate found me, alone and smug in the woods, and taught me that horror really can bite. To misquote the author, "It isn't real horror if it doesn't hurt." In *Those We Left Behind*, Brandon expertly blends fright and pathos to create narratives that are as painful as they are scary, evil little stories that cut you like unseen knives in the dark. The monsters are in control out here, and they will attack you where you're least expecting them. Where you're vulnerable. Where it hurts. If you come out of *Those We Left Behind* unchanged by the experience, then you might be left with the most frightening question of all - are you the monster?"

— Cassandra Yorke, author of *Mary, Everything*

Those WE Left Behind

And Other Sacrifices

BRANDON APPLEGATE

Original cover illustration by Christopher Castillo Díaz

Cover design by Cassandra Yorke

Editing services by Black Quill Editing

Content warnings at the end of the book. Check the table of contents for page number.

Proudly self-published. Visit bapplegate.com for more.

Paperback ISBN: 978-0-578-96839-1
Hardcover ISBN: 978-0-578-96841-4

For Stacey,
who treats this like it matters.

CONTENTS

AUTHOR'S NOTE

Like most works of horror, or really fiction in general, the topics discussed in this book are often not the most pleasant or comfortable. Sometimes it even hurt me to write them down. Basic kindness dictates that I should give you a heads up. So, I've provided **content warnings** toward the back of the book, should you need them. If you don't, well, they're back there anyway.

P.S.: When I write, I tend to think of the story cinematically. One thing of which I'm frequently jealous is a filmmaker's freedom to use both sound and vision to tell a story—particularly their ability to include music. If you want to hear the soundtrack I had in mind to pair with the stories in this book, visit https://spoti.fi/3D9FjJk

FOREWORD

ELFORD ALLEY

The first Brandon Applegate story I read was the titular tale in this collection, *Those We Left Behind*. A story set in space, on Mars to be exact. I was struck by how effortlessly he tossed the reader into this well-worn universe, of men and women working on the red planet in a way that felt true. Just as the sci-fi aspects settle in, you find out there's something waiting just outside of the station in the brown wastes of the Martian surface. Sounds like a familiar premise, but Applegate does so much more with it. Even though there's a monster, that's not how the author frightens you. He won't settle for a rote science fiction tale with a sprinkling of cosmic horror.

No, with Brandon Applegate's fiction, there is always more.

In this collection, Applegate gives us sixteen stories, some interconnected in unexpected ways, but all with a layered and personal approach to horror.

To me, horror works much in the same way as comedy. There is an imbalance in the mundane, it's when the rules we expect to govern our little world break and we're forced to adapt or be destroyed. But in each of these stories, that imbalance occurs with a deeply personal connection, one that elevates the tales beyond what you expect.

Whether these stories take on a cosmic scale or occur within the confines of a dark room, there is an intimacy in them, a solid emotional core. Each protagonist in these tales seems to face a monster born of their own struggles. Because often what scares us isn't actually the ghost in the dark, but the guilt and personal failures that manifested it. Because even when the sun comes up, those fears will not abate. In fact, in Applegate's fiction not even death is a respite.

You'll see yourself in these characters, even if it pains you to do so. In these stories, terror confronts in the guise of loved ones, the gaping maw of a hungry child, or the skeletal hands of a former lover, reaching ever closer.

Some, like *Bedtime Story*, will horrify you. Some, like *You Will Be The One To Find This*, will move you. My personal favorite is *In The Trees*, a story like no other in the collection. I won't spoil them here.

You may not like the places these stories take you, but you'll go nonetheless. You can't help yourself; you can't save yourself.

Enjoy!

Elford Alley
September 1, 2021

INTRODUCTION

THINGS THAT CRAWL IN THE ANCIENT
DARK

If you're reading this, you're an awful lot like me. When it comes to books, you don't skip the extra stuff. You linger in the forewords, the introductions, the prologues, the epilogues. You loiter in the story notes. You meander through the acknowledgments. You savor every last letter on every last page. In short, you're my people.

So, since you're here, I should probably tell you where the stories in this book come from. It's only fair. And, since you're my people, I assume you care about that sort of thing.

We'll start at the beginning.

A little boy tiptoes across his dark living room, stopping to flinch when a board squeaks under the carpet. His knee bumps the coffee table. Glass clinks as something nearly topples and his chest clenches like a fist. He's got to be quiet, and he can't turn on a light. If he wakes his parents and they catch him, they'll send him back to bed and he won't get what he came for.

He's aiming for the kitchen door, on the full other side of the room. During the daytime, when sunlight streams through the windows and noise comes without consequence, he sprints across the space in only a few bounds, but at night, with darkness hugged tight to him like a cloak, it might as well be miles. But now that he's found the table, he has his bearings, and he pads across the remaining distance, arms held out front in case a wall or door—or something *else*—greets him before it's expected.

Things are brighter in the kitchen. The digital microwave clock emits a sphere of neon green light that douses everything in an eerie glow, and there are no curtains in here, so the pumpkin-orange streetlights seep through the blinds and fall on the floor in crooked stripes. The boy tiptoes to the microwave, or rather the shelf beside it. Here is his prize—his mom's stash of grown-up horror books.

There's Stephen King, Clive Barker, Dean Koontz, Anne Rice, and Thomas Harris, all jumping at him like desperate pups in a pound. He spies one he hasn't read yet, snatches it from the shelf, and skitters back toward his bedroom.

This is the hard stuff. He's read all the R.L. Stine, all the Alvin Schwartz he's got and doesn't want to retread. Those are good, and they've been his companions for years, but they're a gateway drug. He's a big kid now, a whole decade old, and while he still eagerly laps up the kiddie stuff, there's something about the stories in the stash. They feel forbidden, taboo. They're full of the stuff Stine can't talk about and his parents won't let him watch on TV. Blood, sex, and dark magic await him in these pages, and the thought of it makes his heart flutter.

He settles into his bed and pulls the covers up tight across his chest. He gets as close as he can to the bedside lamp and lets the story wash over him. He doesn't sleep until the sun rises.

I had a lot of nights like that.

It's that feeling—a mixture of partaking in taboo, of danger and safety all at the same time—that kept me coming back. I had something nobody else around me had, like a secret superpower that helped me cope with life's constant decay.

When bullies pushed me into the gravel on the playground, I went home and read a horror book.

When I left for college and spent my first nights away from home, I read a horror book.

When my wife and I brought our daughter home from the hospital and we stayed up all night, taking turns walking her back and forth, listening to her frantic screams, and trying to figure out what the future held for us, I read a horror book.

I started writing in 2016, during one of the most turbulent periods in my life. My first daughter was four years old, and I didn't know what to do with her yet. Nobody teaches you how to be a dad. As a family, we struggled, always walking a treacherous trail over a precipice of anger and depression, simultaneously clinging to each other and pushing each other away.

You'll see much of that in here. When people ask me what I write about, I tell them "I write about what scares me." But I'm not afraid of body parts coming up through shower drains, carnivorous fairies, or shape-shifting Martians. In these stories, I'm afraid of the choices that lead to them—turning a blind eye to a child's pain, giving in to anger and bitterness, making the wrong decision in a crisis, failing to see what needs to be done. Those are the things that keep me awake long into the night, staring into the blackness, the primal parts of my brain warning me of predators that slink in the corners, and telling me stories about things that crawl in the ancient dark.

And that's where these stories come from.

Some of this is real. Some of this is make-believe. I'm not going to tell you which is which right now because that breaks the spell. If I've done my job here, it's *all* real.

Brandon Applegate
September 21, 2021
Hutto, TX

BEDTIME STORY

The old man settled into the chair beside Danny's bed with a grunt and a sigh. "So, Dan, do you want to hear a story?"

Danny, comforter pulled to his chin, Spider-man pajamas underneath like a suit of armor, looked back at the old man, happier than he'd been in a month. "Sure, Grandpa. What's it about?"

"Spoilers."

Danny scooted closer to the bed's edge. "Is it a scary story?" Danny liked scary stories, even if they sometimes gave him bad dreams.

The old man leaned back in his chair. "Hmph," he said, breath puffing at his gray walrus mustache. "I shouldn't. No, I can't."

"No please, Grandpa, I want to hear it."

"Are you sure?" the old man whispered, sharp like a whistle. "Be sure, because this story is special, Dan. It's all about the truth. It's about the way things really are."

Danny held his breath.

After a silent moment, the old man nodded, blinked, drew in a great lungful of air and began, "Once upon a time, there was a young man. His eyes were full of stars—a bit like your own, come to think of it."

Danny giggled. It had been a long time since grandpa had told him a story. He'd missed it.

"This young man loved his mother and his father and his dog and his friends. He was so full of love he thought he might burst. He believed he was the luckiest boy in the world, and wanted nothing more than to share that.

"One day someone told the young man he could go out into the world and spread love—to save people who needed saving. So he went. His mother and father begged him, pleaded with him to stay, but he wouldn't hear it. People needed him. Evil men had come and taken the families and homes of innocent people who lived far away. The young man believed he could help. He knew it in his bones.

"So, he signed away his life on paper and left his home behind, but not his love. He carried that with him, bright and strong, right here." The old man pointed to his chest.

"In his heart," whispered Danny.

The old man nodded. "He held onto it when they made him run until he threw up, and when they taught him to fight, and when they screamed at him, and when they beat him.

"Then one day they dressed the young man in armor, gave him a gun, and dropped him in the middle of a dark jungle. The young man was afraid. But there, in the jungle, he met more young men like him, and they became his brothers." The old man stopped and breathed deeply, rubbing his eyes beneath his glasses with his fingertips.

Danny thought his wrinkles looked deeper, darker than when he came in.

"It wasn't long," the old man said in a voice like sandpaper. He stopped to clear his throat with a wet cough before he repeated himself, clearer this time, "It wasn't long before the young man figured out he and his new brothers had been tricked. He hadn't been sent there to help. They'd sent him to do terrible things. And he did them—he killed people, sometimes the same people he wanted to protect. He had to watch his new brothers die, too, one by one, scared and alone in the dark, calling out for their mommas and daddies. He wanted to leave, but he couldn't, Dan. Unless they told him he could go."

"Did he get out?" This wasn't like grandpa's other stories. It was scarier, and Grandpa didn't look good. His skin had paled and drooped. Danny hugged his covers.

The old man stared at the window beyond Danny's bed and said, "Not much time—"

"Grandpa?" Danny said, his voice tiny.

"What?" The old man jumped like he'd been daydreaming.

"Did he get out?"

"Oh. Yes. Well, mostly."

Danny didn't ask any more questions.

The old man's cheeks sunk inward. He looked like a talking skull. "Do you know what happened when the young man got home?"

Danny shook his head.

"The people who were supposed to love him deserted him. They said he was a fool. They said he should have known better. They spit on him, screamed at him, threw garbage at him. And when he got to the house where he grew up, his own father wouldn't speak to him." Tears welled in the old man's bloodshot eyes.

Danny cried, too, but held still. "What about his momma?" he whispered.

The old man leaned forward and his bones popped and creaked like wood ready to splinter. "His momma died, Dan," his voice was raspy. "She died in her bed while he ran around in that horrible jungle. His father blamed him, said she died of a broken heart. The young man believed him. There was so much blood on his hands, Dan." The old man stared at his own hands, gaunt, bony, and gnarled like the limbs of an ancient tree. His lips drew back from his teeth in a sneer. "But the world wasn't done with the young man yet. He worked for money, spoke to the right people to get what he needed, but there was no joy, no light left in him.

"During that time, though, he met a girl."

Danny hugged his bunched blanket to his chest. He'd been waiting for the happy ending. Grandpa's stories always had one. Letting out a breath, a wad of tension left his chest.

"Oh, she was beautiful, Dan. Good, kind, and she loved him, too. They were married, had babies, and those babies grew and had their own babies. But he never really got out of that jungle. Every time he closed his eyes he heard the creatures howling in the blackness. When he slept, he heard his brothers' screams. Nobody understood. Nobody wanted to hear about it. He realized he would always be alone with it.

"Then, one day, he looked in the mirror and noticed he was old. His children didn't call him. His grandchildren barely knew him. He'd never told his story to anyone. The world had tossed him aside while he wasn't looking. His whole life had blown by in what felt like an instant.

"He and his wife were alone in a house together, and he was afraid. Because old people die, Dan. They die easily; sometimes of nothing at all. He prayed every day to die before his wife so he didn't have to watch her go. He didn't want to be alone. She was the only person who ever . . . " the old man's voice trembled. "But this life, Dan—this world—doesn't grant wishes.

"When his wife died, the old man was in the living room watching television, of all useless things. He heard her cry out, and when he entered the bedroom, she was lying in the bed wearing her decade-old nightgown, a yellowing paperback book clasped in one hand, her other arm dangling lifelessly over the bedside. She stared at the ceiling with eyes that looked like glass. She'd vomited all over her chest and bedcovers, and the room stank because she'd shit herself."

Danny kept forgetting to breathe. Every muscle in his body locked. The skin on his grandpa's forehead split open showing first pink and grey meat, then white bone underneath. His eyes were cloudy. Where they focused on Danny a few moments before, they now looked blindly into the distance.

"Do you know what he did, Dan?"

Danny did not answer. He shook like a leaf ready to break free from its branch. The old man's skin was turning green and moldy like a troll.

"The damned fool thought he could go with her. He thought for one crazy moment he could have what he wanted. He went to his nightstand, opened the drawer, pulled out his gun,—the revolver they'd sent with him to war—and pressed it to his temple. He looked at his wife, told her he was on his way, and pulled that trigger. He meant it more than he ever did when he killed some fucking rat running around in that damned dark jungle."

Spiders erupted from the old man's wispy yellow hair. They raced onto his face, into his ears. "Is—" Danny swallowed hard. "Is that how you died, Grandpa?" The funeral rushed back to Danny, the bodies in the caskets, painted and motionless. Everyone told him they were his grandparents. He hadn't wanted to believe. But this was his grandpa—he wouldn't hurt him, spiders or not.

Empty sockets looked back at Danny. "Yes," the old man croaked. His mouth hung open and Danny could see his withered stump of tongue. "And they won't let me see her. It's dark where they sent me, and they won't let me see her. But there is a way, Dan. They told me there's a way out. You can help me. I just need to—"

Danny could hear the dry, panicked sob in his Grandpa's voice and pity broke through his terror. "How, Grandpa?" He wanted to help. He hadn't known his Grandpa was so sad, so alone. If he could save him, he'd do it.

"A sacrifice, Dan. A soul for a soul." The old man reached forward, hand trembling, rotten flesh clinging in vain to dusty bones. Bugs crawled and wriggled beneath, bulging the skin and making the palm writhe. The hand extended toward Danny, hung in the air for a moment, then changed direction, wrapping around the stem of the bedside lamp. There was a click, and they were plunged into darkness "There's no reason you have to see…"

Danny tried to speak, but he couldn't. Fear locked his throat up tight. He blinked, willing his eyes to adjust, but they wouldn't. Only his grandpa's labored, phlegmy breath reminded Danny this wasn't a dream.

In the blackness the old man whispered, "Dan, I'm sorry. It's not a sacrifice if it doesn't hurt."

Danny gripped the covers. He wished he could see. His own breathing drowned his grandpa's and his heart pumped in his ears. He wanted to help his grandpa, but not like this. This was too much. A creak sounded at his bedside. Grandpa was moving.

"Mom—Dad," Danny tried to call out but only whispered. He pushed himself upright. He needed to run. A bony hand found his chest and pushed him back to the mattress.

"I'm sorry, Dan." The voice didn't sound like Grandpa anymore. It sounded like a nest of hissing snakes. Skeletal fingers wrapped around Danny's neck and squeezed. "It's the only way."

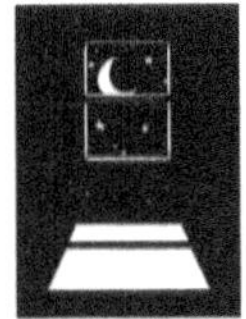

THE PAPER ON WHICH WE ALL
ARE DRAWN

When I was a child, there was a book I wasn't supposed to read, but I did anyway. Inside it was a picture—little more than a scribbled drawing of a black field. I couldn't tell what was night and what was ground or if there was anything else. It was just pure blackness made by a million straight-line passes with a ballpoint pen.

A girl stood in the foreground, a white silhouette sculpted from the night around her, faceless, arms at her sides, shoulders slumped. For all my childhood I knew when I turned to that page in that book, though I couldn't see her eyes, she stared at me, envious. She wanted to come out of the book and be real. If she ever got her wish, I would take her place between those pages, folded away.

It was just a picture.

I used to sit in my bed late at night, my little yellow lamp throwing shadows everywhere, and dare myself to peek through the blinds into the darkness of my back yard. I used to scare myself imagining that when I looked with one eye out into the night the dark would be made up of pen marks, and she would be there. A hole in the universe in the shape of a girl through which I could see the paper on which we all are drawn, the pen strokes crawling up her form like scratches on an old film. She lingered far away but when she saw me watching she drew closer — right next to the window and tapped, wanting to come in. Her sweet voice called to me. Even though my mind screamed I reached for the latch.

I never peeled those blinds apart.

I am grown now, but I still don't look outside at night. I control everything in here. There are lights placed just so. The temperature is always within a degree or two of perfect. There is just the amount of noise I desire. Out there is chaos, nothing, everything. Out there, I control nothing; the wide night air expands like a great outward breath that never ends. I float in it. Beyond is nothing and more nothing, stringing together everything like an infinite strand of the most delicate glass beads. Everything speeds away from everything else. I am small, and all the power, control, safety I feel is a lie. Worst of all, I know she is out there, a thinning of the membrane between what we see and what we cannot see, an embodiment of negative space.

Tonight, I will look.

I am in my living room alone. My daughters are asleep. We have had a day full of screaming and fighting and loving. My wife is asleep. She has been sad recently. I know it's my fault. I don't do enough. She cries when she thinks I'm not looking. Lingers too long in closets, bathrooms, assuming I don't see. She doesn't want to hurt me, but I know nothing turned out the way we planned.

I am tired of being a disappointment. It's such a mistake to put all your happiness in someone else's hands like she has in mine. I am clumsy and don't know what to do with breakable things.

I step in front of the big window in my living room. We always close the blinds at sunset. I trace them with my fingertips, then slip my finger under the slat and pull, revealing a sharp black line. I lean down and look through with one eye like I imagined.

She stands next to the swing set. I gasp at the reality of her. She doesn't have eyes, but I feel it when she sees me, like a moth landing on my nose. She walks forward, arms hanging limp. Through her, as she approaches, between the scratchy pen strokes of reality that give her form and shading, I see things for what they are. Even nothing is something, even space is filled with existence and possibility. On the other side of her, what she shows me, is truest nothing. A vacuum, but less. The pure, white blankness has seen me, seen us all, and waits infinitely patient to consume blindly, thoughtlessly.

My eyes grow wide. She is at the window.

"The time has come to let me in," she whispers, her voice as sweet as in my dream.

I reach for the latch.

TEA PARTY

"Dad, we can't stop yet. We'll be late for the tea party."

"I know, baby," Albert says. He lets her hand go and stops running, doubling over, trying not to make a show of catching his breath. "I just need a minute." His chest is tight, and his legs are on fire, but he's happy because they are together.

Maddie smiles, and her eyes dance, pinpricks of light doing pirouettes against her irises. Last week, he thought he'd lost her, but everything will be okay now. He can see it in her eyes, in her face. He can hear it in the musical waterfall of her laugh. He gets to have his little girl again.

"Daddy, my friends don't like to be kept waiting."

Albert hears something he doesn't like in her voice, but he can't place it. It's something about the way she said *friends*.

Maddie steps closer to him and puts her hand on his shoulder. "We're almost there," she whispers.

Albert nods and inhales deep; his lungs burn. He straightens up with some effort. "Okay," he says. "I'm all right. Can we walk, though?"

Maddie's face screws up in a grimace.

Albert can deal with disappointment—he expected a tantrum. Maddie retakes his hand, and they walk.

For the first time since they entered the woods behind their home, Albert looks around. He never comes here; he's always viewed the woods as beautiful to look at but uncomfortable to experience. Sweat builds on his skin, seeping into the fabric around his crotch and below his paunch. Grime coats his face. He itches in places he doesn't like to scratch when people are watching.

The path folds and turns often enough during their trek his sunlit yard has disappeared. The forest drew itself around them like a curtain, grass and leaves encroaching, erasing the trail. Tree trunks like obsidian columns tower into a green luminescent canopy. Sunlight pierces open spaces where motes drift and bugs flutter. The colors are too bright, surreal, fantastic. Shadows in the foliage are deep and hollow like holes in the world.

"Tell me about your friends," Albert's voice shakes in a way he doesn't expect. He clears his throat. It's likely Maddie carried a few teddy bears and toys off into the woods somewhere, maybe into a little clearing, setting them up on the ground or around a stump.

"Well, there's Michael, and Margaret, and Phillip." She counts them on her hand.

"Ouch!" Albert slaps at his forearm. Something bit him. Or maybe pinched him. He hates the damned woods and every bug in them.

Maddie gasps, stopping short when she hears the slap. She looks up at him with panic in her eyes. Then her gaze drifts and follows something up and away from him; her brows unravel and relax. "I told you to wait," she says, staring into the trees over Albert's shoulder.

"Excuse me?"

"Nothing," Maddie says, her eyes darting back to him. She smiles too big.

Albert recognizes the smile, and it stops him cold. She's hiding something. He shivers.

"You sure?" That guilty grin chills his blood.

"What?" Maddie's big eyes twinkle in the swaying light.

This is going nowhere—a brick wall. It's always about plausible deniability with Maddie, an expert negotiator since she could speak. Someone with an innate sense of when to talk, when to clam up, and how to use semantics. She's backed him into a corner more than once. Albert has learned that the key is not to engage, not to allow her to build a case. This often means stopping the conversation before he wants to. "Nevermind," he says. "Let's keep going."

They walk in silence. Albert's muscles relax, the soreness in his legs tolerable, but he doesn't mention it, or Maddie will make him run again. As much as he wants to reach their destination, have the tea party, then leave, he doesn't think he can run much more.

Something big buzzes past, reminding him of the dragonflies he used to bat away when his father took him fishing. He turns his head but doesn't see it. Then, it lands on his neck, and another sharp pain fires down his spine.

No mistaking it, that was a bite.

Tiny teeth tore a bit of his flesh away.

"Son of a bitch!" Albert slaps his neck. Tacky blood coats his palm. He reaches back, and his fingertips find a little hole in his flesh.

Maddie stares at the ground near his feet, lip quivering, eyes welling as if she might cry.

Albert looks down and sees the path, some loose rocks, strewn leaves.

Maddie screams. "Phillip!" Tears streak her face.

"What? Who's Phillip?" One of the friends she talked about? Imaginary? Maybe. Shouldn't she be growing out of that? "There's nothing there, Maddie," he says, as much for himself as for her. Maddie's emotions don't need to be his, too. He needs to stay calm.

"You killed him!"

Albert flinches, and hopes Maddie doesn't see.

Maddie dives to the ground and scoops something in her cupped hands. She holds up her empty palms to Albert like an offering. A snarl twists her mouth, her face red with fury and grief. "You killed Phillip!" She stands, balancing to keep from dropping whatever she thinks she's holding, then carries it off the path. Kneeling, she opens her hands on the forest floor. "I told you to wait," she whispers. Her tears patter on the dry leaves.

Albert's eyes fill with tears. This isn't real, but it's real for Maddie. "Baby." He steps toward her. "I'm so sorry." Albert squats next to her, puts a hand on her shoulder, and tries to pull her into a hug.

She jerks from his grasp, then turns her face to him, eyes ablaze. She winds back and slaps him hard across the cheek.

Albert cries out in shock.

"You *asshole*! You always take things from me."

Albert scrambles backward on his palms. He shouldn't show fear, but the heat comes off her in waves.

"You take everything!" her scream echoes off the trees. Birds flap their wings, fleeing from the unexpected outburst. "First Mom's gone, and now you murdered Phillip!"

Albert bursts into tears. He doesn't want her to see him cry. It seems like an admission of guilt, even though he has nothing to feel sorry for. But this proclamation from Maddie—he'd always suspected she felt that way about her mom, but her bluntness catches him off guard.

He summons his nerve and forces a stern expression. "Maddie, that's enough. Come on. We're going back to the house." It's time to end this. He wants to regain control of the situation and he can't do that out here in these unfamiliar woods.

They're in deep, too far from the yard, the house. He's off-balance.

"No!" Maddie jumps away from him, but Albert moves fast.

He grabs her wrist and yanks. Then she's on her knees in front of him. Albert stands and tightens his grip. He expects her to yelp, but she doesn't. She pulls back, looking for weaknesses in his hold, rotating her hand and wrist. She's slippery, and his palms are slick with sweat. She yanks her arm free.

"Maddie, now!" his voice is a bark that bounces off the hulking tree trunks. He wishes his wife was here; she always handled this kind of thing better.

Maddie's on the path, a blazing fury, her shoulders squared ready to rush him. Albert locks eyes with his daughter. Her mouth has twisted into a sardonic grin.

"Take him," she says through gritted teeth. "We'll carry him the rest of the way."

"Wha—"

Something flits past.

He turns but sees nothing. Something else, or maybe the same thing, buzzes by his face in the opposite direction. Tiny gusts from its wingbeats blow across his skin. His breathing quickens and the short, sharp gasps coming from his mouth ramp up his heartbeat. *What is this?* He hears them, feels their fluttering, only showing up at the edges of his vision, fleeting blurs and shadows circling.

"Maddie, we need to go," his voice is pleading. He reaches for her.

Something jabs his forearm like a needle.

Albert yelps as another one stabs his neck. Sticky blood flows from the pinpricks. Then they're everywhere. They crawl up his legs. Creep into his clothes. Fly, dive, flit around inside his shorts. Hot pain shoots up from between his legs. Something bites into his scrotum. Albert howls. He runs, swatting at himself. Teeth, pincers, stingers—maybe all of them—jam in deeper.

He's left her. Left his Maddie behind in a cloud of biting bugs. Why isn't she following him? Have they swarmed her? She's not screaming. He should go back—what kind of father would run away like this?

His legs won't let him turn back. Little shadows dart around him. They form a cloud—a swarm. The air buzzes. They attack his shirt, shredding fabric. They crawl inside and bite his back, chew up his skin. He's off the path. The forest whizzes by. His head bounces off the tree trunk with a crunch.

Maddie's laughter drifts down from the branches as he lies flat on his back. His vision bursts with stars, blinking out fast. Even in the coming darkness, her voice is beautiful, a flute-like song from a glass harp. He closes his eyes, surrendering to the numbness that overtakes him, and lets the sound carry him away.

MADDIE HAD WAITED FOREVER FOR IT TO BE SPRING IN THE little forest clearing. The woods have always been green, but today they're electric, like sour apple candy. Flowers erupt from the ground, scattered in patches like little rugs that glow pink and red and blue and white. It's as if they're celebrating. Running water burbles over stones from a nearby brook, and the birds sing to its rhythm, flitting and chasing one another above her head.

The real show is up there and Maddie watches. Orbs of light, from blush to cobalt, each about as big as a gumball, dance among the frolicking birds and perch on the overhanging branches in the canopy. This is their home, and they've welcomed Maddie in, told her she belongs with them—or will soon. It's why she can see them. Oh, how she wants to be like them. Delicate, powerful, dangerous, free; they are everything she dreams of being. That's what today is all about. She kept her promise, and they will keep theirs, but for now, she watches them: rainbow-hued twinkles spiraling and darting and stopping to rest.

A teal light darts down from the tree branch and floats for a moment, like a leaf, before settling on her shoulder. Maddie calls him Michael, although he has never given her his name. His feet tickle the bare skin at the base of her neck, above her shirt collar. She keeps her head still, afraid to smash the delicate creature, even though she knows he's too fast. She tilts her head away, assisting Michael as he scales her neck like a mountain, scrambling over her jawline and pulling himself into her ear.

"Drink up," he says.

No matter how many times Maddie hears him talk, she expects him to squeak like a cartoon mouse, but his voice is always soft, whispery, barely distinguishable from the breeze and trickling brook.

"You must eat and drink everything we give you if you want to join us."

Maddie nearly forgot the table before her, a massive stump sliced through at the right height, its surface a scar healed and hardened by time and weather. Sitting on it is a plate—a large leaf with a small sandwich on top—the surface around it covered in breadcrumbs. A teacup, expertly carved from knobbed wood, sits beside the dish, and beyond them, an ornately carved wooden teapot. Michael's teal light jumps from Maddie's shoulder and then flies down to the table. For a moment, Maddie sees the creature clearly, all char-black gangly limbs and wild, bulbous eyes that glow so bright they're white in the middle. Its tangle of minuscule, needle-like teeth remind her of a picture she once saw of a deep-sea fish. Its transparent insect wings beat so fast they're invisible. She looks away until Michael has flown a good distance; they are horrible creatures, and she has no desire to get close to them until she transforms. She has decided once they share the same hideous aspect, they'll frighten her much less, or at least she'll get used to them. If nothing else, the benefits will outweigh the drawbacks.

Michael swoops down to the table, into the teapot's looping handle, then flies upward, lifting the pot and tipping it into Maddie's cup. A thick, dark liquid oozes from the spout. Maddie doesn't know what it is—certainly *not* tea—but it tastes like peppermint and is grainy like mud. It's not altogether unpleasant. Michael sets the pot back down. Maddie raises it to her lips and tilts her head back, letting the viscous liquid dribble onto her tongue, relaxing her throat so she can more easily drink the strange elixir. The ache in her bones, the tingle in her skin herald the coming metamorphosis.

Michael scoots the plate toward her.

Maddie grins. "You are so impatient."

The little teal light urges the plate closer, insistent.

"Very well." She heaves a little sigh at the creature, a ghost of a smile on her lips. She sets the cup down on the stump and lifts the little sandwich to her lips. The bread has green and white spots on it, but Maddie ignores them. She opens her mouth and bites down, feeling the crunch then a warm squirt. Some juice dribbles from her bottom lip and gathers in the divot above her chin. She tongues the sandwich to the back of her mouth then chews, crunching it like a lollipop. Politely, she covers her mouth and giggles. "Oh, Michael, the finger sandwiches are just divine."

But Michael has flown away to join the others, swarming around another guest at the table. Her father sits across from her in a chair made from a hollowed trunk. He stares off into the trees, eyes dull and cloudy. His jaw hangs slack, drool mixed with blood stringing from his bottom lip and pooling on his chest. He's piled into the chair like a ragdoll, his limbs flaccid and awkward, his skin dotted with red pinpricks. His forehead is bloody mush. A twinkling fuchsia orb by his hand rends free another finger with a twig-like snap and a fabric-like rip. Her father's body twitches. His eyes grow wide, and his breathing speeds up, then slows. The fairies—she's decided that's what they are—like their meat fresh and their blood warm. They burrow into the spine and brain, immobilizing their prey but keeping them alive as long as possible. In this state, he'll feed them for days.

Maddie stares in awe and wonders if he still recognizes her. Does he still know who I am? Is he still in there, trapped? Paralyzed? Does he know what's happening? She hopes so.

The bright pink light lifts the detached finger onto a piece of moldy bread, then folds the slice in half over it. The fairy picks it up and flies it toward Maddie, dropping it on her plate.

"Thank you, Margaret," Maddie sings as Margaret flies away.

She thinks of her mother—he said he couldn't do anything about that, but he's wrong. She thinks of Phillip, impatient, hungry, lying dead on the dirt path. I hope you feel every bit of this, Dad, for everything you've taken from me.

Her bones don't just ache now; they hurt. She's shrinking, changing. Her shoulder pops and shifts as she crunches the last of the sandwich between her back teeth and reaches for the next one. Soon she'll be small enough to properly join in the feast.

Maddie laughs, a flute-like song drifting through the branches. She wonders again if he can hear.

THE LAST DAYS OF THE
OLD MAN

Clay inhaled the smoke, and when he breathed it out, he imagined himself as a dragon. He contorted his face in a monstrous snarl as the smoke curled up in front of his eyes.

"Oh, Smaug the Mighty," said a deep voice with a heavy drawl from behind him. "Not gold alone brought us hither. I'd take a smoke, if you've got one to spare."

Clay jumped. "Jesus fuck, Merle." He turned to look at the old man approaching from behind him. Hunched, messy, white hair, yellow-white beard, mustache grown out to cover his thin lips. His boots were dusty and worn. The crepe-paper skin around his eyes split open to reveal sun-narrowed slivers of the brightest blue Clay had ever seen.

Merle was the proud owner of the only independent bookstore between Houston and Austin that wasn't feverishly trying to sell to the highest bidder. The old fool must have a printing press in the back cranking out some seriously convincing counterfeit hundreds to keep paying the rent.

Merle let a mischievous chuckle climb out of his chest and leaned against the brick wall next to the door. "Jumped like a damned scalded cat, boy. That ain't reefer, is it? Shit'll make you paranoid."

Clay narrowed his eyes at the old man and slid a pack of Pall Malls out of his jacket pocket. He flipped open the cardboard top and offered the open box to his boss. "No sir," Clay said. "It's the really bad stuff."

Merle sniffed and pulled a butt from the box. "Cheap, too."

"Picky." Clay took a drag. "Weren't you gonna be a writer, old man?" Clay knew the answer, but he liked to hear the old man talk.

"Something like that," said Merle, not looking up.

"What'd you write about?"

"Wizards and monsters and dragons and kings."

"Doesn't seem right, an old cowboy like you."

"Ain't always been an old cowboy," said Merle. "Ain't nobody ever *always* been one thing."

Clay nodded. Fair enough. "Got any of your work still sitting around?"

"You don't want to read my old shit."

They finished their cigarettes in silence before returning to the cool, brown dark inside the shop. Clay took up his post on the stool at the wood bar-top counter. Merle disappeared into the back and didn't emerge for the next several hours.

Clay made a sizable dent in his book, not to mention the Pall Malls, before he saw the old man again. When Merle did show himself, he seemed to materialize from the shelves. The shop had a way of muffling sound, and no line of sight in most directions except from the register to the front door. If it weren't for the colors on the books' spines, the place could double as a sensory deprivation chamber. So, when Merle stepped into his peripheral vision, Clay let out a startled yip.

"You seem a little high-strung." Merle's blue eyes shone like chrome through the slits in his eyelids and his mouth turned up at the corners, trying and failing to stifle a smile. "Maybe you ought to take some time off from all this stressful work I'm having you do around here." The old man gestured widely to the shop with his empty left hand. His right hand stayed at his side cradling a thin leather notebook like a surprise.

Clay eyed the notebook and grinned. "I wouldn't leave you by yourself, old man. You'd probably work yourself to death without me. Then who'd pay my rent?"

Merle flicked his wrist and the notebook slapped onto the bar top. "If you still want to read it, there it is. That's where it all started." He looked down, then turned, avoiding Clay's eyes. He opened his mouth like he wanted to say something else, closed it again, then walked off as suddenly as he'd appeared.

Clay stared at the notebook on the counter. A tingle of excitement built in his chest and the air seemed to vibrate around his ears. He must have had that same conversation with the old man a dozen times over the last couple years. It always ended the same way, with Merle waving a dismissive hand at Clay and grumping back into the store. What changed? Clay looked off in the direction Merle had gone. The tight row of shelves was as deserted as ever.

Clay wandered off from the shop at around four, after checking that the old man was alright to lock up. Merle lived in the back, on a little cot surrounded by towering stacks of books that looked even older than he was.

He drove back to his apartment with the leather-bound notebook in his lap. It vibrated with an invisible energy. Clay chalked that up to adrenaline. He couldn't remember the last time he had been so excited to read anything.

He swung the old Nova into a parking spot and jumped out, almost forgetting to slam the car door behind him in his rush to bound up the steps into his apartment.

It was a plain, boxy one-bedroom on the second floor, with shitty neighbors above and shitty neighbors below. The only furniture were a flatscreen television, a Playstation that sat in the middle of the floor, wires strung across the ratty old carpet and disappearing behind the particle board TV stand, and a curb-trash couch so darkly colored at least two lifetimes worth of stains were hidden. A green and blue glass bong sat conspicuously on the kitchen bar top. The walls were spattered with band posters and show fliers affixed to the sheetrock with thumbtacks.

Clay swerved and slalomed past his possessions on autopilot to the bedroom where he threw himself down on the mattress on the floor. The springs squeaked.

The notebook cover was worn, aged leather, unmarked by writing. Clay turned to the front page which read: *On The Nature of Magic*, in handwriting he recognized from the store's ledger. Wide-eyed, he ventured to the first full page and read:

FEBRUARY 24, 1920

I have not left this library for three weeks by my best count as well as that of the grandfather clock in the corner by the infuriatingly unlocked door. Not to piss, not to eat, not to see the sun. The clock chimes as loud as a church bell at noon and at midnight, every single day. So, I can hardly fail to keep track. I have opened the door many times. I would only have to take a single step out of this room and into the next. I am perfectly capable of leaving. If I do, I will die, because I am supposed *to be dead.*

I am tethered by a speck of dust. It is a speck whittled away from a rock which was part of the original matter that exploded from the instantaneous point of perfect, unstable near-nothing that preceded our universe's creation. The speck, or as I have come to call it, The Point, is one of the oldest pieces of matter in existence, and located less than three miles below this room, embedded in the Earth's crust. If I or any other living thing were within a mile of it we would be incinerated, or, more accurately, shaken to pieces small enough to dissolve into the surrounding air and eventually into the quantum fabric of the universe. It vibrates the floor beneath my feet like distant machinery. It's halted my aging and keeps my heart beating, channeling its great power through me. In return, it demands my protection.

I must escape.

I have never been a social creature, but still this room's silence is maddening. I miss food. I miss whiskey. I miss cigarettes. I miss people. But this is a library, and there are books, thousands of them amassed by previous occupants and they all deal with the manipulation of reality's fabric by either forgotten, arcane means, or hoarded knowledge not yet discovered by mainstream humanity.

Magic.

That's how I will leave this place and still live. I will find a way to sustain my own life without having to rely on The Point.

WHEN CLAY LOOKED UP FROM THE NOTEBOOK, THE SKY glowed gray with new sun. By his watch, nearly thirteen hours had passed since he'd first flopped onto the bed and begun to read the notebook. He closed it and held it up in front of him, examining its spine and edges. It was about the size of a store-bought spiral notebook, yet Clay had not, in all that time, read the same page twice. The pages, written in Merle's tight, angular cursive—more like sword strokes than pen strokes—read like a diary.

What followed that first entry were recipes for a hundred different potions, concoctions and draughts, hand-drawn diagrams of runic symbols and designs, incantations, and passages in languages Clay not only didn't understand, but could not identify.

These things were interspersed with dated diary entries, from 1920 through October 1923, dealing mostly with failed attempts to escape from the library but occasionally with fending off an attack on The Point by various deities and mages.

The entries stopped with no apparent resolution.

I see why nobody published this, Clay thought. Still, it fascinated him. He could still remember the book's pages with intense clarity, like in old movies when somebody rolled through microfilm in a library.

By the time Clay got dressed, the sun hung over the treetops and was baking hot. This is what he imagined it to be like inside a cremation oven: yellow, oppressive, persistent. By the time he parked the Nova in his spot on the street, the air rippled with heat.

The door to the bookshop was shut and locked. He could see through the glass that the lights were out. Odd for this hour; Merle always propped the door open at first light. He said it gave the place a chance to air out before customers showed up. Of course, the place never really aired out, and there were never any customers, but Clay didn't say anything.

He unlocked the door and pulled it open. Hot air erupted from the shop and hit Clay in the face. "Shit. Merle?"

No answer came.

Clay toed the metal doorstop down against the pavement and flicked on the light switch. He took the center path through the store, heading straight for the counter at the back. He'd check the bathroom, Merle's room, and the alleyway out back. Maybe the old man stepped out for a smoke.

The store was deserted.

As he came out of the back room, Clay caught sight of a silhouetted figure—a tall, thin man framed in the propped open front door. Clay stopped. "Help you?" he said.

"I know it's early," the man said in a silky, quiet voice that did not seem powerful enough to travel the shop's full depth. "Are you open?"

"We open at eleven," said Clay. "We're still setting up." He turned toward the alley door and found himself rooted in place.

The tall man's boots *double-thunked* on the hardwood floor with every step. He slowly strolled up to the counter, absently perusing the books on the shelves on either side as he approached.

"Can I help you?" Clay repeated with a grunt, trying and failing to lift his foot from the floor.

"I'm looking for something—specific," said the tall man. "*Obscure.*"

"What's on the shelves is what we've got," said Clay, forcing his voice into a disaffected tone, hoping to play the bored employee long enough for the man to leave. Then he could continue his search for Merle.

The tall man arrived at the counter and dropped both long-fingered hands casually on the bar top. How had he fit through the front door without ducking? He must be at least seven feet tall. He wore a slick black suit, exquisitely tailored so it seemed almost a part of him. His face was pale and gaunt, but not old, and his eyes were sunken and dark.

He looked around and clucked his tongue as though deciding what to order from a menu. "I'm looking for," the man dragged out each syllable as if toying with Clay, "something called *On The Nature of Magic*. It's an odd volume. Only one copy ever produced, in fact. I believe the proprietor of this shop wrote it. Have you heard of it?" On the last sentence, the man ceased looking around him and focused his hollow eyes on Clay.

"Not sure I know what you mean," Clay attempted to speak calmly but his voice jumped up an octave. "If you come back later when the old man is here, I'll bet he can help."

The tall man chuckled and it sounded like dry leaves rustling. "Old man," he said, shaking his head and looking down at the bar top. "Boy, you have no idea."

"What's your name?" Clay asked.

"Excuse me?" said the tall man, raising his eyes.

"Can I get your name? For when he gets back. So I can tell him you came by."

"Giddeon," said the man. "Arthur Giddeon. Actually, the old man and I have already had one chat this morning. He seemed to think he had sent the book beyond my reach. Laughable old idiot. I have come here for the book and I *will* leave *with* it. I also intend to make it worth your while." Giddeon tapped his long, pale fingers on the counter. One-two-three-four. One-two-three-four.

Giddeon—a mage from the book; he'd once tried to attack The Point.

No way, Clay thought. "Look, Mr. Giddeon," he said, putting on his best bored-Taco-bell-employee expression, "I don't know what you're talking about, and if Merle didn't give you the book this morning, I don't know what to tell you. Now if you don't mind, I've got to finish opening up the store. We open at eight if you want to buy something else."

Clay felt his airway constrict, and his feet lifted off the ground. He found himself unrooted, floating toward the ceiling. Giddeon's eyes were rolled back into his head, only the whites showing. He made a strange gesture with his right hand, his bony fingers unnaturally bent.

Clay bumped into the ceiling. His hands were forced out to his sides and held fast against the rafters as if bound. He opened his mouth and closed it like a fish out of water.

Giddeon spoke gruffly, through clenched teeth, "Show me where the book is now, boy, or I will turn you inside out like a plastic bag."

Clay's vision wavered and darkened at the edges, his lungs screamed in agony. Without thinking about it, the book flashed through his brain, spinning and landing on random pages like microfilm. He could read them. There, that one. With the last bit of his air and strength, he made a gagging sound to signal he wanted to speak. The pressure on his windpipe released, but he stayed pinned.

"You wish to say something?" Giddeon said.

"Yes," said Clay in between deep gasps. "I was trying to say . . . you should not have . . . given me . . . your name."

Giddeon's eyes widened, and he forced his hand into an even more contorted gesture. Before the stranger could do what he was planning, Clay recalled the page he wanted from the book. A wind gust swept around the shop. Loose paper scattered and books toppled off shelves. Giddeon's eyes rolled back, revealing black irises and he dropped his hands, clearly expecting Clay to fall. Clay, however, stayed put. He held out his hands, twisted them into odd, painful shapes and mumbled something rhythmic in a dead tongue. Then, much more loudly, he said, "Giddeon."

A blast of air shot from the back of the shop and hit the tall man in the torso like a battering ram, throwing him down the center aisle and through the propped-open front door. Clay swiped his right hand. The door slammed shut and the deadbolt turned. He floated to the floor. The wind still circling the shop died down and then stopped.

Merle's gonna kill me for this mess. Clay laughed, then sprinted for the back door that led to the alley.

He burst into the sunshine and, there, sitting propped against the blue, rusting dumpster, was Merle. Blood soaked his shirt. His eyes were closed. As Clay approached, they cracked open. "You read the book," said Merle, "or you'd be as dead as I am."

"Jesus fuck," Clay said, squatting down next to the old man. Merle had been old as long as Clay'd known him, but it was like the shop owner had aged fifty years in a single night. His skin barely clung to his bones. Clay started to lay a hand on his arm, then recoiled, afraid he'd break him. "What the hell's going on?"

"Put some hoo-doo on it so you'd remember what you read," Merle said, mostly mumbling. "Did it work?" He looked over Clay's shoulder at the sky.

"Yeah, I'd say so."

Merle smirked. He pointed past Clay to the other end of the alley with an ancient, shaking finger. "Then you'll know who that piece of shit is."

Giddeon limped, bleeding, around the building's corner and onto the gravel alley. Pivoting to face him, Clay held his arms out to either side to protect Merle. "Stay away from us!"

Giddeon stopped twenty yards away. "Do you think I am afraid of dying? Afraid of an old man and his *intern?*"

"Maybe you ought to be," said Clay.

Behind him, Merle let out a dry chuckle that turned into a

cough wet with blood.

"You don't sound too good, old man," said Giddeon. His boots crunched in the gravel as he slowly approached.

"Stay where you are," Clay said.

"Make me," said Giddeon with a twittering laugh.

"Boy," said Merle softly, kicking Clay's ankle. "You got a smoke?"

Clay, scrolling through the book in his head, searching for something useful, looked over his shoulder at the old man. "*Now*, Merle?"

"Pretty sure I'm gonna be dead in a minute. Now or never."

Clay reached into his shirt pocket, pulled out the Pall Malls, and tossed them to Merle. They landed on the old man's chest.

Clay turned his attention back to Giddeon and contorted his fingers. The wind picked up. This one will have to do, Clay thought, I've got no time to keep looking.

This time, though, Giddeon was ready. The wind that blasted down the alley did not so much as ruffle his suit. A steel trash can tumbled toward him; he deflected it with a wave of his hand. "The first time was a lucky shot, boy," Giddeon said. "Now you're pissing me off."

Merle's lighter clinked.

Clay was gently pushed to one side by something he couldn't see. His sneakers skidded, leaving trails in the gravel. He looked behind him and saw Merle struggling to his feet.

"That's all right, boy. I've got one more in me."

Giddeon laughed, a sound like shattering glass.

Merle took a long drag of the Pall Mall and held the smoke in his lungs before dropping the butt on the ground and stubbing it out with his toe. His eyes rolled back, he brought his hands out in front of him, and clapped once. Every glass pane in every window in the alleyway shattered.

Clay covered his ears.

Merle opened his mouth. An animal growl escaped his throat. Smoke drifted out of his mouth in lazy tendrils. The air in front of his face wavered with the heat of the fire that emerged from his lips. A military flamethrower, in a cone that swallowed Giddeon.

Clay could do nothing but listen to the screams and shield his eyes from the white-hot flames.

Everything stopped.

Merle staggered backward and fell, hitting his head on the steel dumpster, which rang like an out-of-tune bell. A spurt of blood slopped from his soot-caked lips. He gestured for Clay to come to him, but the boy was already sliding through the gravel next to him, a runner making a play for home plate.

"Merle, that was crazy."

"Got the idea from you yesterday." Merle grinned, revealing blackened, bloody teeth. "Smaug the Mighty."

Clay barked out a laugh. "Are you gonna be all right?"

"Nope—this is it for me, boy."

Clay pulled his phone out of his pocket and dialed nine.

Merle put a hand on his wrist to stop him. "No."

"We've got to get you to a doctor."

"Ain't no doctor gonna fix what's wrong with me. And to be true, I don't want them to. I been waiting a long time to rest."

"Because of me?" said Clay. "Why me? Why did you give me the book? Why am I special?"

"You ain't." Merle let out another wet cough. "But neither was I. We was both just . . . there. Wrong place or right, it don't matter. Only thing that *does* matter is what you do with it. To my mind, you've got some work to do."

"The Point," Clay murmured.

Merle nodded. "Giddeon ain't the only one after it, and they'll split the Earth open to get it. Will you . . ." his voice faltered, his eyes unfocusing, dilating. "Will you—" Merle's head lolled to one side. His mouth hung slack. His hand lay heavy on Clay's wrist.

A sob rose in Clay's throat, he pushed it back down. He had work to do.

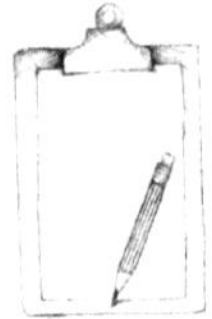

ROOTS RUN DEEP

Harland was chewing on a big bite of sandwich when the singing started. He swallowed it down and reached for the walkie. "Suarez? The hell is going on down there?"

He never got an answer.

Teams searched for days but never found the twenty-three members of Delta Crew. But the singing never stopped. Management dictated a channel switch for all on-site radios, but Harland still changed over when he was alone and tried to make out his friends' individual voices. Sometimes he thought he could hear Suarez—that gorgeous, unwavering baritone.

HARLAND PRESSED A BUTTON AND DROPPED INTO THE EARTH.

"Tell me again what they were doing." The man from OSHA was bookish, short. His voice made Harland's teeth grit.

"We'd just completed a blast, trying to break into a seam further down," Harland shouted over the elevator's racket.

The OSHA man nodded and looked at his clipboard. "Why weren't you with them? You were the shift supervisor, right?"

How many times was he going to have to answer that damned question? "Pretty sure that story is already in the paperwork."

"Early lunch," the OSHA man said.

The elevator shuddered and banged into the shaft floor. Harland opened the gate. The two men disembarked and stood silent in the center of the cavernous first chamber.

Harland held up a finger. "Do you hear it?"

"What?" The OSHA man looked up.

"The singing."

They held their breaths. From up the tunnels floated a sweet harmony of voices.

"It's like a choir warming up," Harland said.

"I've heard this before. The blast uncovered a hole that's open to the surface. That's the wind blowing through it—like a flute," The OSHA man's voice trembled, unsure.

"Could be," said Harland. "Suppose you'll want to see the blast site."

The OSHA man nodded.

"It's a long way down." Harland motioned for him to follow.

THE MINE WAS A MASS OF WINDING TUNNELS THAT ZIG-ZAGGED downward through the earth. Wire hung on the walls like streamers between the sodium-vapor lights. The two men traveled in silence, alone except for the voices.

Harland had been down here often since they shut the mine. At first, he eagerly participated in the search parties, but when those went unsatisfied he came down on his own, laid in the center of the blast site, closed his eyes and imagined his smell. Suarez always smelled of cologne under the sweat and dirt.

"How much further?" The OSHA man was sweating. The singing was loud and he held a palm to his ear.

"Just around this turn."

The blast chamber was bigger than the tunnel behind, with craggy walls where the explosives ripped stone from stone. Debris was swept into piles around the room.

"This is it," Harland said.

The OSHA man ran his fingers over the wall. "This is where they disappeared?"

"Yes."

"I thought there'd be an opening or something. I don't even know what I'm going to write—hey, what's this?" The OSHA man fingered at something in a crack.

"Roots," said Harland. He'd noticed them during the first search party and examined them at length. There were hundreds of the little brown protrusions—maybe thousands.

"But that's—what's growing this far down?"

"No idea."

The OSHA man continued around the perimeter. "They're everywhere. Why didn't you mention this in your report?"

"Didn't seem important," Harland said, his voice quavered. "They're strange. You should put your hand on one."

The OSHA man stopped and pressed his palm over one of the nubs. "It's warm—is it—" He jerked his hand away, but Harland, who had moved closer behind him, forced it back against the wall. "What are you doing?"

"Can you feel it move?" Harland's eyes blazed.

"Y—yes."

The OSHA man struggled, but Harland was strong. One hand held the inspector's wrist, flattening his palm against the wall. The other arm wrapped around the inspector, pinning his arm to his side.

"There are only a few species of carnivorous plants in the world. Almost all of them eat bugs. This one is different. Best I can figure, these roots subsisted on rats before we scared them all off."

The OSHA man screamed. A red rivulet trickled down the

wall from beneath his palm. His arm shook and jerked, but Harland held him in place.

The song rose to a mad, expectant cacophony.

"It's inside me! Please help me!" The OSHA man trembled beneath Harland's hug.

At first, it was like the veins in the inspector's arms had come alive, twisting beneath his skin, up to his elbows, his biceps, his shoulders. The tendrils gathered in ringlets and shot buds up through the skin. They crawled up his neck, toward his spine. He jerked. A glottal cry escaped his blanched lips. "*Hrng—*"

He began to sing. The OSHA man's voice was a beautiful tenor. Other roots extended from the wall, wrapped around him and embraced him to the rock. He no longer fought.

"There!" Harland screamed in the echoing chamber. "Are you satisfied? Will you open for me now?"

There was no answer but the song, seeming to delight in its newest voice.

"Show me!"

The floor rumbled beneath Harland's feet. He stumbled and thrust his arms out to his sides, keeping his balance. Golf ball-sized chunks of rock shed from the walls all around and clattered to the floor.

Oh god, a cave-in. Harland didn't want to die buried in this claustrophobic hell-pit. The OSHA man's dangling limbs swung like a marrionette's, but his sunken eyes, half-lidded, didn't react. He just sang, nearly screaming, over the thunderous roar.

With a lightning *snap*, cracks exploded in the wall behind the OSHA man like a sunburst. Tendrils of root snaked from the fissures and curled like great ropy fingers that gripped the wall and pulled. The rock receded like a stage curtain parting, and the OSHA man disappeared, carried off into the darkness beyond, a doll in a massive hand.

The shaking ceased and the singing returned to its less fevered pitch. Harland approached the yawning stone mouth before him.

He'd found the source. His friends were inside. Suarez was inside. He held his breath. Determination gripped him, pushing away the terror that tried to crawl up the inside of his chest.

He stepped forward. Blackness swallowed him. The singing blared, louder in here. He could make out each voice. Thick root strands pushed the stones back into place behind him, closing the entrance and snuffing the light from the corridor. His heart leaped, and he stopped. His instincts willed him to turn and run, find a gap while he still could and claw his way to freedom. But, no. It was no use. Not even a sliver of light leaked through from the chamber beyond. And now that he was here, he couldn't leave them. He felt the wound on his index finger. A root had bitten him during the first search party. He knew then where the crew had gone—and what he had to do.

He pulled the flashlight from his belt. The dark ate the beam. The song throbbed in his blood. Bulbous creepers undulated at his feet. He walked, groping for anything other than black air.

The flashlight found it first: a wall of pulsing roots, woven like a squirming wicker barricade.

Harland slid the circle of light along the roots until it met a man, or what was left of one. The staring eyes were sunk deep into the skeletal face, the mouth dropped open. A falsetto note flowed forth in piercing perfection. Beneath the clasping vines that held the figure to the wall, the stomach was concave, the chest striated with exposed ribs. *Davis.* Harland's stomach turned and he continued along the wall.

He passed four more emaciated, singing bodies before he found Suarez. He would have missed him were it not for the baritone—Suarez's deep voice resonated with his skin.

Harland pulled the knife from his belt. With one hand, he grasped a vine that looped around Suarez's chest. It writhed in his palm and Harland suppressed a gag. He raised the knife and hacked it. The blade hardly made a mark. Harland bared down with his whole weight. It wouldn't cut. A frustrated scream burst from his throat. He swung the knife again. The blade bounced off the root and sliced Suarez's chest.

There was no blood. Instead, the skin bulged. A cluster of tiny tendrils snaked from the cut, each tipped with a tiny, snapping mouth. They reached, sensing Harland's closeness.

He fell backward, crying out. There was nothing left inside Suarez. Nothing but these—things.

What had they uncovered? It hardly mattered. Everything Harland cared about was here.

They'd only kissed once, a stolen moment behind the office trailer. They were afraid to be found out—but there was nothing left to fear. Harland stepped close, placed his palm on Suarez's chest. He leaned in and covered Suarez's mouth with his own. The song pulsed in his throat, lips crumpled like dry paper.

Roots crawled from Suarez's mouth into Harland's, tentatively at first, exploring. The mouths at the tendrils' ends lapped at the moisture inside his cheeks, on his tongue. Let them come. They crawled down his throat in choking spirals. His eyes bulged, then rolled back into his skull.

When the roots filled him, he and the man he loved sang as one.

THE GOAT MAN

Matt rolls the old Ford up to the bridge, but doesn't cut the lights. It looks the same. But everything out here does. Fifty years later, and it's like stepping into a memory—the most exquisite sensation of deja vu. The past blends into the present out here in the open air. It dances in front of him, playing like a movie. He fingers the grip of the gun on his belt.

If the Goat Man won't do it this time, he'll do it himself.

CREEDENCE BLARES. THE PICKUP'S TIRES SKID ON GRAVEL. Maybe the whole thing will tumble off the road. Maybe Matt's blood will pour out onto a cow pasture and he'll die there, alone, staring into the grass. He doesn't care. Anything would be better than going back and getting the shit kicked out of him by his old man.

There's the bridge. It's not what comes to mind when he imagines something haunted. It's a flat concrete pad connecting two banks of a little stream. Barely any room for a man to scramble underneath on hands and knees. He's not surprised to find out the jerks at school are full of shit. Nothing lives under there.

Matt chugs the beer that's now warm from sitting in the fork of his crotch then flings the empty bottle out into the night. He takes his foot off the brake and lets the truck roll forward. The instructions are very specific: park on the bridge, cut the engine and the lights, then honk three times. That's when the Goat Man comes out and carries you off. Nobody knows what he does with you, but Matt's drunk enough not to care.

The Goat Man's nothing but a boogeyman. The real threat is everything else.

He stumbles out of the truck. The night has the same effect on him as a library or a church—the reverent need to be quiet stifles his desire to scream into the blackness. Silence sits heavily, wrapping around him like a cloak. Pasture stretches out all around. Stars blaze like blue fire. The world is monochrome. Out here, everything is big, the whole night stretches to the universe's end like a great sigh and he's a speck floating on the current.

The Dodge's engine ticks behind him as it cools. He slams the truck door and leans against it. Reaching in through the open window, he finds the button on the wheel, honks once, and winces at the sacrilegious loudness of it. He quickly does it twice more. The sound rolls outward then dies on the breeze. Matt holds his breath.

This is stupid. He's drunk and avoiding going home, that's all. "Are you there?" his shout cuts the night. "Do you want me, Goat Man?" That's it, isn't it? Nobody wants him. He's a burden. Daddy tells him that daily—every time he puts a fist in his gut. Everyone at school avoids him like the bruises are contagious, like the dirt on his clothes will rub off and his misfortune with it.

A rustling sound draws his attention to the ground in front of him. Something black scrambles onto the bridge's lip. It flexes, looking for purchase. Is it a rat? No, it's—

Matt's guts freeze. It's a hand.

A shape claws its way up onto the bridge, blacker than the night around it, dripping wet from the creek below. The water patters underneath as it crawls on all fours into the road. It stands on two legs like a man, but its hair and beard are wild like an animal. Its eyes hide in shadow and its rotted lips peel backward in a sneer. The figure raises an arm and levels its clawed hand at Matt. When it opens its mouth, a series of wet, gagging grunts issue forth. Is it trying to speak?

Something primal unhinges inside Matt. He came with the idea of giving himself to this creature, but now that he's seen it, his instincts for self-preservation are stronger than his angst and self-hatred. His legs move on their own. He sprints for the truck, flinging the door open and diving inside. The thing staggers toward him. It lets out a chittering scream. Matt thrusts the key into place. The pickup roars to life. He averts his eyes. Doesn't want to look at the thing in the headlight glow. It's gnarled, outstretched hands nearly touch the hood. Matt throws the truck into reverse and stomps the accelerator to the floor.

Gravel explodes in all directions. Matt leans into the wheel. He yanks it. The truck spins, scrambles for purchase, then flies.

Matt doesn't look in the rear-view until he's on the freeway.

IF HE HADN'T BEEN SUCH A CHICKENSHIT FIFTY YEARS AGO, none of this would have happened. Darla would've ended up with someone better—or at least he wouldn't have been to blame. He wouldn't have become the kind of monster he'd been desperate to escape.

He cuts the engine and bails into the dark on the bridge. Every second since he fled from this place has been cursed. He thought when he left town things would get better, but they didn't. He left a trail of broken lives in his wake. His daughter, his wife—they'd both paid the price for being his. Maybe his little girl still has a chance.

If he feeds himself to the Goat Man, gives back what he cheated the creature out of, the old hex might lift. The drugs will let go of her, and so will that junkie boyfriend. He's been living on borrowed time, and she's paying the interest.

He reaches through the door and blasts the horn three times into the night. "I'm back, you old goat! Come and take me!"

Matt waits for a long time. The engine in the Ford stops ticking. The crickets, silenced by the horn blast, resume their song.

Goat Man ain't coming. That's okay. He can still atone. An old sadness overtakes him, shakes him to his bones. He pulls the pistol from his belt and presses it against his temple. He can't even think of any last words. It hardly matters. Nobody will be there to hear them.

A crack, a flash, a spatter of blood. Matt tumbles into the creek.

HE WAKES TO THE TINKLING OF WATER. HIS EYELIDS SPLIT painfully open and he stares up at something flat and gray. Stone? Is he underground? It's so close over him that he can't turn. He tries to move his legs, his arms, but every joint flares with bright white agony. How long has he been here?

An abrupt sound makes him jump. A car horn—one long blast and two shorter ones. He's under the bridge. The whole thing comes back to him: He shot himself. Did he somehow fuck up something as simple as blowing his own brains out? And now there's some kid up there on the bridge waiting for the Goat Man. Jesus.

"Are you there?" a kid shouts then says something else but Matt can't make it out over his own labored breathing.

He reaches up, grabs at the bridge's edge, and drags himself up from the trickling creek. The kid's gone silent. Matt's cheeks flush hot with embarrassment.

With both hands he hoists himself onto the bridge, every inch of him simultaneously freezing and on fire, and crawls on his hands and knees out into the road. He's never felt his age like this before. His joints crackle and snap.

His pickup is still on the bridge. A figure stands in front of it, stock still. But—wait. That's not *his* truck. At least not the one he came with. It's the old Dodge he bought when he was seventeen. But it can't be. His daddy sold it for beer money a week before he graduated. He hasn't seen that truck since the last time he was out here. The silhouette in front of it . . . Matt's eyes take a moment to adjust to the moonlight, but when they do . . . He knows that face.

This changes everything.

The boy stares back at him, mouth agape, eyes bugged. Matt stands, despite the pain. He reaches out a hand to tell the boy— what? That he's in danger of becoming his father? He wants to tell him to get help, to learn how to show kindness and be satisfied. Most of all he wants to tell the boy there is no Goat Man, and certainly no curse. Everything that happens from this point forward hinges on his choices. He wants to tell the kid to take accountability for his own actions—he can do better. He sees it in the kid's face; there's still *potential* there, something the years stole from his own aspect. He's got to get this kid to move, to change. It's the only way to stop what's coming.

All that comes out of his mouth is a watery croak, then another.

The kid turns on his heel and runs, stumbling back to the truck.

Matt tries to call him back. The scream tears at his vocal cords, but no matter how hard he tries to form words, his tongue remains a shrivelled mass in the back of his throat. He can't force his lips together. Staggering forward, he puts every ounce of strength he has into catching up with the boy. It's futile.

The Dodge sprays him with gravel as it spins in the road and howls away.

He stands in the dark for a long time, staring at his rotten, moss-covered hands. He'll never leave this place. But he never really did.

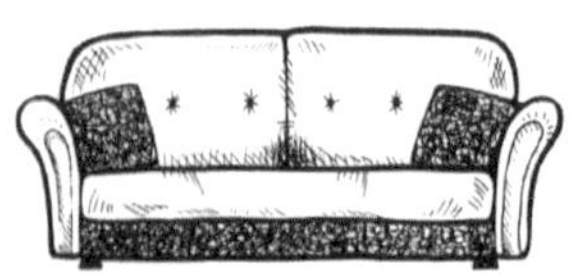

A LITTLE BREAK

"You're sure you'll be okay without us?" Tam asks, cocking one eyebrow up and smiling with one side of her pink mouth. She knows the answer. She's draped in comfortable clothes for driving, backpack slung over her shoulder, hand on Maggie's neck.

Maggie is seven, staring up at her dad, frowning. Will stands inside the threshold, leaning a hand on the doorframe in a move he hopes comes off as casual indifference, but looks more like he's trying to block his family from coming back inside. Margo, the baby, is already strapped into her car seat. They only have a couple minutes before she gets tired of being alone and starts to holler.

"You know me." Will smirks. "Mister alone-time."

"Why aren't you coming with us, Dad?" Maggie asks, part earnest, part cloying. "Don't you want to see Granny Sarah?"

Will winces. He looks down at her bigger-than-they-should-be green eyes and takes a knee. "Baby." He puts a hand on her face, runs his fingers through her hair. "Of course I'd love to see Granny Sarah. It's just—"

"Daddy just needs some time alone once in a while. It's how he recharges his batteries," Tam interrupts.

Will furrows his brow and shoots his wife a split-second glance, hoping she doesn't notice. He hates it when she explains his excuses. He returns his gaze to Maggie, sees her pained expression and realizes what he must look like. All thunder and petulance. He covers his bad mood with a forced smile.

The tension drains from Maggie's face.

"I like to have a little break once in a while to keep my batteries... from... run . . . ning..." Will mimes a robot and drops his voice an octave.

Maggie giggles.

Tam's cynical smirk breaks into a real smile.

This is better. This is how you do it. Will looks up at Tam. "It's a day. I think I can manage."

Last hugs and kisses, be carefuls and love yous are exchanged. Maggie hugs Will like she's trying to break ribs when he lifts her tiny body off the ground.

The car disappears around the corner. Will swings the door closed, hears the latch snap into place and ceremoniously turns the deadbolt. He listens to the blessed, soothing balm of silence.

WILL FELL ASLEEP ON THE COUCH. HE CAN STILL FEEL IT underneath him, cool leather and soft stuffing, but even with his eyes closed he knows he is outside. The sun warms his face. A breeze carries the smells of dry spice and damp rot. Leaves rustle. The wind rumbles in his ears. The only thing missing is birdsong.

He opens his eyes, still doubting his other senses. He stares into a bright blue sky streaked with wispy clouds. It's framed by the black treetop silhouettes that lean over him like concerned bystanders.

Will should be afraid, but he isn't. He raises up on his elbows and looks around. He's in a clearing. Dark forest encircles him, chokingly thick, all black and green and brown with no cracks for the sky to shine through. It is solid as a wall. He has the sensation of sitting at the bottom of a great black bowl. A mosquito lands on Will's arm, its whining unnoticed until it falls silent then drinks deeply through his skin. Will slaps it, smearing blood across his bicep.

Only then does Will see the man standing in the tree line. Too tall, angular, wearing black robes that make him look like a shadow cast between trees. A crown made of jutting antlers tops his head. Will would have mistaken the man for part of the forest were it not for the deathly pale face glinting from beneath his hood. Will squints, leaning forward on the couch. The man raises an arm, and a single finger beckons. Will stands without thinking.

One step forward. Another. Dry grass and parched dirt crunch beneath his feet. Will cannot say why he obeys, only that he feels pulled. As though there are strings attached to that finger, compelling him like a marionette. Will's vision blurs for a moment. When it clears he stands directly in front of the man.

The man's arms must be six feet long. Will's eyes follow the man's torso up to his antler-crowned head. His father's face stares at him from beneath the black hood.

"Fuck." Will wheezes, his throat suddenly dry.

His father's lips lift in an unnatural smile, all angles and teeth. His arm bends upward with two separate elbow joints and reaches into his robe's collar, fumbling for something.

Will is unable to move or speak. He's not sure what has him pinned in place, whether it's simple fear or the strange power flowing from this man. The hairs on his arm, his face, vibrate with some charge in the air.

The man, Will's father, finds what he is probing for inside his robe and tears it free with a wet snap, pulling his hand out from underneath his collar. He takes a knee and the great white moon of a face is only inches away.

His father lifts his bony white hand until it hovers at the edge of Will's vision. The man holds a human heart, red, wet, and still throbbing, empty and gasping for blood to move. Will locks his eyes with the ice blue ones in that death-white face. The grin fades and the lips move. In a voice that sounds like it is made up more of the vibration in Will's skull than any organic voice box's machinations, the man says a single word:

"Eat."

The T in *eat* becomes a drawn out static hiss. The world buzzes. Will's hair stands on end. His skull pulsates. His eyes roll back into his head and he sees red and then black.

THE WORLD IS BLESSEDLY STILL, BUT THE MEMORY OF THE pulsating energy that shook Will's skull, numbed his skin, clings to him like a spider's web. Will's eyes are closed. The leather sofa cushion is cool beneath him, and the air conditioner's hum reminds him he was dreaming and has awakened safe in his living room.

Unpleasant memories flood Will's mind. Groggy, he drags himself into a sitting position. The windows are black rectangles. He has been asleep for hours. It felt like minutes.

Will gets up, stumbles before finding his footing. The floor is cold on his bare feet. The kitchen is only a few feet away and he decides he needs food. And a stiff drink. Definitely a drink. He heads for the liquor cabinet.

He's been dry since his father died a few months ago. He didn't stop drinking on purpose, he just hasn't felt the need, but that dream has him scrambling for a shot glass. He pulls one down from the cabinet and fills it to the brim with vodka then tosses the clear liquid down his throat. The gasoline fumes clear his sinuses before his throat constricts and he coughs. When the fit subsides, he stands with his hands on his bent knees and stares at the floor. He pours another shot and knocks it back. This time there's no coughing.

A pleasant warmth travels up and down his body. For the first time since he woke from that horrible dream, his muscles relax. He flops onto the couch again, ambitions of feeding himself anything other than Grey Goose forgotten. He pours another shot and this time, before downing it, he raises it into the air in front of his face. "Ol' Art," he says, and then, as he moves the glass toward his mouth he adds, "Go fuck yourself."

With the third shot down, his scalp tingles. There's a muffled need to piss, but he intends to ignore the impulse for as long as he can.

That son of a bitch never let go entirely. Fathers never do. Will remembers Maggie's face when things got tense at the door earlier. There's something frightening about a father. Children know on some primal level that Daddy might sooner eat or abandon them than stay and raise them. Will often wonders, based on his own impulses, whether modern fatherhood is an unnatural state, something artificial. But that's his own daddy talking.

He didn't live with his old man for long. Art left when he was seven, the same age as Maggie. Then, in high school, Will moved in with him for a little while after a row with his mom. He showed up on Art's door holding a duffle bag and smoking an American Spirit. The first time Will had seen his father in nine years and all Art did was look him up and down, say "Put that out," in his cold, level voice, then walked back into the house. He left the door open, though, so Will went in.

Art kept to the basement, only emerging for food. He never ate with Will, never cooked, just came upstairs, grabbed something in a box or a can then went back downstairs. In those moments when the door to the basement stood open while Art dug around in the pantry, Will walked to the basement door and peered down. It was dark, but sometimes there was a dim glow he could only see once his eyes adjusted—sometimes blue, sometimes green, sometimes red. It illuminated shapes slithering on the concrete floor. And it *stank*—a mix of gasoline and burnt electronics and a smell Will remembered from when his dog had crawled up under the porch to die and they hadn't found him for a couple weeks. Then boots clomped along the wood floors, from the kitchen. Will would skitter back to his couch in the living room and pretend to watch television. Not that Art noticed. He just closed the door behind him, locked it, and clomped down the stairs.

Will went back to his mom's place after a few weeks. If his father ever called to check on him, he didn't know about it.

Then, about three years ago—Maggie was four at the time—Will heard from his mom that Art was in a retirement home in Round Rock. Tam insisted they go see him, that it was important for Maggie to know who her grandfather was, even if she didn't *know* him. They fought hard that night. Will's mind kept returning to the undulating shapes in the dim red glow on the concrete basement floor. He couldn't tell Tam about it— she'd think he was crazy. He wasn't even sure of himself when he thought about it. If he looked straight at the memory it faded to something more mundane.

In the end he acquiesced. The doctor at the home, Dr. Hart, had told him Art suffered from dementia, though when Will looked at his father, the old man looked as sharp as ever. He didn't even look that old. When Will walked through the door of his small white box of a room, Art looked at him with instant recognition, and something like distaste. That expression changed when Tam and Maggie came in behind him. He lit up like Christmas, and by the end of the short visit he was calling Maggie his "little turtledove."

A couple weeks after the visit, a patrolling cop found Art facedown and sunburned in an alley about twenty miles from the retirement home. Dr. Hart said he had "gotten out," like a dog or something.

"Sometimes patients at this stage of dementia wander off." The doctor shrugged, offered rote condolences and asked if there was anything he could do.

Will waved him off. He felt such relief at the funeral he

refused to eulogize his father for fear he might laugh.

Two more shots down. He doesn't feel it right away, but Will knows when he stands he'll be tipsy. He lurches off the couch, intending to go to the kitchen for snacks, but when his stomach turns, he continues into the hall instead, bouncing and dragging his shoulders on the walls toward his bedroom.

He flops down on the bed, head spinning, muscles glad to be relieved of the burden of his weight. He sinks into the mattress and keeps sinking until shadow swallows him and he looks up toward the bedroom ceiling like his bed is the surface of an icy lake and he fell in a hole in the ice. But the water is warm and cradles him and his head's spinning rocks him into a stone dead sleep.

THERE'S A BREEZE AND THE SOUND OF LEAVES RUSTLING. WILL is back in the dream, in the clearing. He doesn't taste the alcohol in his mouth anymore, doesn't feel his head buzzing, and so there's no way in hell this is reality, because those five (or was it six?) shots hit him like a truck.

He opens his eyes and sees stars between the encroaching trees. Night has fallen in the forest. His mother used to say, "There's nothing in the dark that's not there in the light," but Will always had a feeling that was bullshit. Here, doubly so. Slithering sounds float up from the ground around his bed. The forest rustles and cracks. Will sits up. "Is this going to be a nightly fucking thing now?" he grumbles aloud, not expecting an answer. He rubs his forehead with the heels of his palms. Then he says louder, toward the tree line, "Art, are you out there again?"

Art's not standing at the tree line this time, but walking along inside it, like he's stalking prey.

"Art!"

The figure doesn't react, only keeps walking. It stops when

it's aligned with Will's footboard. His father's face turns toward him, then fades back into the shadows.

Will swings his feet off the bed, then he recoils. Some sort of slug-things, black and shiny like fish bodies, writhe over and under each other, weaving a carpet on the grass. They're the same things that slithered around in his father's basement.

Will's stomach turns. He knows instinctively what it's like to touch them. They glop and stick like slime eels. When he puts his foot down it touches wet grass. The slug things slither quickly away, forming a circle around where he stands. The circle moves with him as he walks. A force pulls will toward the tree line. The tree trunks turn shiny and slick; they look like those slugs, and they undulate. As he enters the trees, Will keeps his hands close to his sides to avoid touching them.

Everything is black. Will navigates by the feeling in his chest pulling him through the tree trunks.

Will stops. He is in another, much smaller clearing. A roof of limbs weaves together above him, blocking out the starlight. The slug things are not in this clearing, but they slither in the trees. The gigantic robed thing with his father's face under those massive antlers ducks under the lowest rung of tree canopy and moves toward Will. It spider-walks on its hands and feet. Art's face does not smile. It looks at Will with something like hunger.

"This way," his father's face says.

Will shudders. "Jesus Christ, is that actually you, Art?"

The robed thing grunts in the affirmative.

The unseen force drags Will across the clearing toward his father. "What the fuck is going on?"

"I am tired of being here," the Art-thing says. It turns to Will and grins, showing double rows of sharpened teeth. "You will help me leave."

"Wait, did you bring me here to kill me?"

"No, boy."

The figure in front of Will crumples and flattens as hundreds of the slug things pour out of its robes. It flops onto the ground like laundry. The slug things swarm across the ground forming a black river running toward Will's feet.

He tells himself to turn, run, but the command dies in his brain stem. He watches, eyes bulging from their sockets, heart threatening to explode in his chest. His breath hisses in and out so fast he's sure he'll hyperventilate and he begs for it, *Please let me pass out or die before that gets here.*

He does not.

When the slugs reach him, they split open to reveal circular maws filled with spinning rows of teeth. The first of them slithers onto the top of his foot, leaving a wet trail in its wake that's cool in the night air. It turns its face down and suctions itself like a leach to Will's skin. Will's heart hammers. Why can't he move? Why can't he scream? Every muscle, tendon, and sinew from his neck to his ankles is frozen, locked. More of the things are on him, wriggling into position. The spinning teeth drill into him, churning his skin like earth for planting. Oh, how he wants to scream, to fall to the ground and flail, anything to relieve the bright, hot agony boring into his feet and legs. They're inside his pants, his shirt, entering him. They're inside his skin, crawling beneath it, pulling it away from his muscle and boring deeper, finding bone, coiling up around it.

Then he moves. For a moment he thinks he's beaten the magic that holds him in place, but he takes a step forward that he didn't intend to. The slugs inside him move him like a puppet, forcing him to stomp toward Art's empty, discarded pile of skin.

Another clump of slugs emerges from beneath the black, rubbery mass. They're carrying something—a beating human heart.

"Eat."

Art's voice comes from inside Will, vibrating his bones.

Will struggles to stop his arm from reaching down and picking up the heart, but the signals sent from his brain simply don't reach his limbs. His fist closes around the beating organ and he lifts it to his lips.

"Eat."

The slugs open Will's jaw. His teeth sink into the tissue. Hot blood spurts like tomato juice. His throat opens. A slick lump of flesh slides down. Will's gut churns. Please let me stop, he thinks. He eats until all that's left is the tacky blood on his palm.

THE CAR PULLS INTO THE DRIVEWAY.

Bright yellow sunlight pours through the windows. Will spent the morning cleaning up for their arrival. Tam will be pleased. The car doors slam. Maggie chatters to her mother in the driveway. The voices get louder as they approach the door. He waits for Maggie to press the doorbell as she always does before he opens it.

"Daddy!" Maggie cries and flings herself at his legs, encircling them in a hug that speaks of much more than a day apart.

Will smiles and reaches down to pat her back. "Hello, my little *turtledove*," he says, his right hand tightening around the handle of the butcher knife behind his back.

Maggie lets go of his legs and Will steps aside to let them in. They make their usual racket—baby Margo crying, Maggie jabbering about Granny Sarah, Tam sighing and rolling her eyes at Will, but smiling.

No, not this, Will thinks. They're my family. They're your family, too.

The little one will taste sweetest. I'll save her for last. Art's voice croaks in his skull.

"No." The word comes out of Will as little more than a breath.

"What babe?" Tam turns and asks.

"Nothing, my love." Will smiles wide.

"You okay?" Tam cocks her head.

"Of course. Probably just a little too much time on my own." He closes the door and follows them into the house.

ELEVATOR

There is a man on the elevator when we get on. Mickey recoils immediately, but I'm not surprised. He's seven and shy. He scrambles behind my leg. I tousle his hair, then step us both backward so the man can get off.

The man doesn't move. He's middle aged, face craggy like a split rock, stubble growing patchy like moss. His eyes are gray, milky like he's blind, staring right at us. The smell of dirt and body odor bubbles out of the elevator. The man looks at me, then Mickey and gives him a small smile and a wink. I gesture as politely as I can for him to come out. He looks at me again and stays still. His smile disappears.

I try not to let my face betray my nerves. I push Mickey forward onto the elevator with me. I turn him, facing us both toward the doors, placing myself between him and the man.

The lights on the button panel are dark. "What floor?" I ask, packing my tone with as much good will as I can.

The man doesn't speak, but I hear him breathing.

I look back over my shoulder. "What floor?"

He only stares at me with those storm-cloud gray eyes.

The elevator doors slide closed. I pick twelve, my floor, and grip Mickey's shoulders tighter. His muscles tense under my palms and I wonder if I squeezed too hard or if he's nervous. Maybe both.

The man never moves. The red numbers above the button panel count up slowly, like the elevator is deliberately taking its time. I look back at the man and he's smiling at Mickey again, teeth bared, eyes wide. He doesn't notice me. Panic wads in my chest and I turn away.

Floor seven. I stare stubbornly at the doors. I don't want to look back anymore.

Floor nine. My knuckles are white as I grip Mickey's shoulders. If it hurts him, he doesn't say anything.

Floor eleven. The man's breathing has gone quiet, like he's holding it.

The elevator dings like a pealing bell and I flinch. Cold tingles race along my skin. When the doors slide open I shove Mickey through them and he stumbles out onto the elaborate hallway carpet. I jump off after him.

I turn around to look at the man, suddenly terrified he will step off with us. I scream, stumble backward a few steps.

There is nobody on the elevator. Nobody in the hall.

The doors slide closed and I dart forward, stopping them with my hand. I look up. The roof panels are not disturbed. Can people even get on top of elevators that way? I've only seen it in movies. I step back and let the doors close. Look left and right. The hallway is deserted except for Mickey and me.

"Are you okay, Mom?" Mickey asks.

"Sure, honey." I take deep breaths, try to slow my heart. When I feel more myself, I turn Mickey toward our apartment. "Mickey . . ." I hesitate. He doesn't look at me. "Did you see that man in the elevator?"

"Of course." Mickey shrugs.

The thick carpet muffles our footsteps. We walk the rest of the way to our apartment in silence. While I dig in my purse for the key, a question occurs to me. I think about the way the man smiled at Mickey. I stop digging and pause. "Mickey, have you ever seen that man before?"

"Yeah."

I feel cold. "Where, baby?"

"In my room," Mickey says. "He likes to watch me sleep."

IN THE TREES

The Texas summer shone yellow with dust and sun. Daniel was eight years old and lived on a triangular plot of land, two sides of which were bordered by oak woods, tangled, gnarled, and parched. The bottom third was road, hot, dark, flatter than the earth was supposed to be and more dangerous than a rattlesnake. More than anything in the world, Daniel loved the wood and hated the road.

The wood loved Daniel in return.

As with all things in Texas, the trees, still green and full from the boon of spring, stood defiant against the baking heat. In this defiance and patience Daniel found a kindred spirit.

When Daniel was free from school and the intrusions of friends, he walked in the woods and talked to the trees. They sheltered him as best they could from the heat. The boy and the trees held out together until Daniel could take no more and went back inside with the manufactured cool air and made plans to try again tomorrow. On these occasions, the trees of the wood expressed their disappointment.

"You can't stay a little longer?" they whispered. "You can't stand a little more?"

"No," Daniel said, disappointed in himself, hanging his head and watching the ground as he walked back. He wished he were a tree so he could weather the heat and live for a thousand years.

One day he sat down between the roots of a particularly gnarled, old tree at the center of the wood to rest. "I wish I were a tree like you," Daniel said.

"Why do you wish to be anything other than what you are?" the tree's voice was a raspy whisper like sticks rubbing together.

"I'm small and weak, and humans don't live very long," Daniel said.

"But you have dominated so much of the earth," said the tree. "Surely you are strong, for your kind have felled many of mine."

"We make tools so we can cut down even the tallest tree."

"Ah, but surely you grow large, because you take up so much space," said the tree.

"That's only because there are so many of us," said the boy.

"Then you must be long-lived, because when you cut us down, you never give us the chance to grow back," said the tree.

"That's only because we pass our property and our stories from one generation to the next, so they know how to use the tools. They also take up too much space."

The tree was silent for a long time, and the more it thought about what the boy said, the angrier it became, until it vowed not to speak any more, at least for that day.

When Daniel realized what had happened, he said, "I'm sorry." He left the wood with his head hung low not because he wished he was a tree, but because he feared he had destroyed an irreplaceable friendship.

EVERY NIGHT WHEN DANIEL WENT TO BED, HE LISTENED TO his parents as they fought. They never spoke to each other while Daniel was awake, but when they thought he was asleep, they whispered things that sounded like painful secrets. This escalated into hushed voices, and Daniel, staring at his wall in the blue moonlight, could make out a few words. "Beer" and "money" and other words he'd been told were only for adults. After several long pauses, thumps, and slamming doors, his parents would scream at each other.

Sometimes, if he tried hard enough, Daniel could be asleep before this happened. On this night, though, his conversation with the tree kept him awake and worried. Those fears smashed together with his parents fighting so he couldn't sleep no matter how he tried.

Tonight, when the screaming started, it was louder, more desperate than usual. Daniel shook beneath his covers. Sounds he hadn't heard before accompanied them—a sharp, meaty *thwack*, followed by a scream and a thud.

The scream belonged to his mother.

If Daniel loved anything more than the wood, it was her. She was gentle and kind. She protected him. When she punished him, it was mild. Daniel always believed it was because she loved him. That scream, short, like a mountain lion howl, had been angry and laced with real pain.

Daniel's heart beat so fast he could feel it in his fingertips. All the same, he knew what he had to do. She would do it for him.

Daniel snuck out of bed.

One foot and then the next, he tip-toed across his bedroom, down the hall. He stopped before he entered the kitchen. The lights were on. His mother sobbed quietly.

"Shut up!" his father's voice danced around the kitchen in too high an octave.

Daniel stuck his head around the corner and saw his father. He raised his hand into the air, golden ring glinting in the fluorescent kitchen light, and arced it back then shot it swiftly toward Daniel's mother's pink, blood-streaked face.

Daniel flinched. His mother let out a bark of a scream from where she sat against the wall. She sobbed, her left eye purple and swollen, and wiped her bleeding nose on her shirt sleeve.

Panic seized Daniel. He pulled in as much air as he could and held it, his lungs burned. He looked around the room for a way to stop this. A hot tear crawled down his cheek. In the corner next to the dining table lay his father's tool belt. Daniel's father always discarded it there when he came home from work, usually on his way to the fridge for a beer. Daniel's eyes scanned the pouches.

The hammer.

Daniel scrambled across the floor and snatched the tool from the belt, pivoted, and made a bee line for his father.

Daniel's mother moaned. "Oh, god."

"Leave her alone!" Daniel swung the hammer blindly.

His father had time to turn his head toward the unexpected noise. His eyes were unfocused with drink, his movement sluggish. The hammer made contact with his kneecap and something cracked, moved in a way it wasn't supposed to. He toppled and hit the floor, injured leg shooting out in front of him, head flopping to the side, making a loud *thunk* against the refrigerator door.

Daniel stood, stunned, unable for a moment to process what he had done. He looked at his mother. Her one open eye was red with fear and tears. Blood oozed from her nose and split lip.

"Oh, baby, no," she said.

Just then, his father's massive hand swiped at Daniel's face.

"Go," Daniel's mother said.

Daniel flung himself to his feet and sprinted. He hit the screen door hard, flinging it open, and his feet hit the grass before it slammed behind him. When he was at the edge of the lawn, his father stumbled onto the front porch.

"Daniel!"

Daniel flew toward the wood.

The trees were different at night. They whispered. On a

normal day Daniel stopped to greet them, but not tonight. The murmurs from the leaves became more frantic.

Daniel ran so fast his tears were swept back across his face and into the hair above his ears. Leaves crunched beneath his feet. He raised his arms to protect his face from whipping branches but none came, as though they had been deliberately raised out of his way. Daniel said a silent thanks.

"Daniel!" his father's voice sounded behind him, echoing, distant, crazed.

Daniel doubled his effort. He knew the land and his father did not. That might be an advantage. He was also faster and didn't drink, but his lungs ached as they emptied and refilled with damp night air. Each breath became more shallow, not going as far as it had before.

His father's clumsy bootsteps got closer.

Daniel looked over his shoulder, trusting too much in the cleared path ahead, and slipped. He went down hard, his t-shirt seam tearing as a dead branch snagged cloth and skin. He lay on his back and smiled. This was exactly where he wanted to be.

"Friend!" Daniel shouted up at the massive old oak in the wood's center.

The tree said nothing.

"Please listen," Daniel said.

His father's crazed shouts bled through the trees, ever closer.

"Say what you must," whispered the tree.

Daniel got up onto his knees. "My friend, please, protect me."

"From what?"

"My father is angry. He's looking for me and he's going to hurt me!" Daniel looked back over his shoulder.

The tree paused for a long moment, then said, "Surely a boy of your kind has nothing to fear from his father."

"He's drunk," said Daniel, "and he already hurt my mom."

"You must have done something to wrong him," there was

petty anger in the tree's whisper. "Who am I to stand between a boy and some much-needed discipline?"

"Please," Daniel said. "Just let me climb up into your branches to hide."

"Surely you have some tool at your disposal you could use to protect yourself. Your kind have felled many of mine. One of your own should be no problem. Or is it that you'd like to give your father a reason to cut me down as well?"

"I'm sorry," Daniel said through sobs threatening to choke him. "I know you're mad at me, but I need your help."

"No," said the tree.

Daniel, too tired to run more, too afraid to scream, too small and weak to fight, turned his back to the tree and leaned his weight upon the solid trunk. He felt its warmth through his shirt and his mind ran away for a moment to days spent running and playing. A calm settled over him and he smiled in spite of his situation. He said up to the tree, "It's okay. I know I hurt you and that you are angry, but I'm still your friend, and I know you're mine. I'll sit with you until this is over."

The tree did not answer, so Daniel waited.

Out of the woods in front of Daniel came a monster. His father, stumbling drunk and bare-chested, dragged his nearly dead leg behind him. He was covered in cuts and bruises from the branches he had run through. Daniel took satisfaction in thinking that at least not all his friends had abandoned him. His eyes, kind or worried when sober, blazed with green fire fueled by hate and drink.

"Dad," Daniel said. "I'm sorry."

"There you are." His father's eyes darted around as if looking for anyone watching.

"Dad, I'm sorry I hurt you. I love you. Please don't."

But Daniel's father did not answer. He dragged himself, grunting, toward Daniel, one step at a time. When he got to Daniel, he reached down with both hands and picked Daniel up under his arms. He stood the boy on his feet, pressed his back against the tree, and wrapped his shaking hands around Daniel's throat. As he squeezed he screamed.

When his son stopped moving, he dropped him on the ground. Daniel lay against the tree's giant gnarled roots.

"Are you the boy's father?" a voice whispered.

"What?"

"How could a father do something like that to his son?"

"Who's talking?" Daniel's father spun in a circle, stumbling, eyes darting.

"Is he dead?" several voices whispered.

A chorus broke out all around him. They asked questions he didn't know how to answer, didn't *want* to.

"No," he said. "The boy's fine, he'll get up." Daniel's father looked at his son, crumpled on the ground by the tree root, small and helpless as the day he was born. "Get up, boy. Dan. Daniel. Get up."

"He will not get up," the big oak said. "I can't feel his heart beating in my roots. I always could before."

"What? No." Daniel's father swatted at the air around his head. "Who's talking? Where are you? Get up, Daniel. We need to go home."

"You killed him!" its voice sounded like a saw through a log. "You have murdered your boy—my *friend*!"

"Murderer," the other voices said. It became a chant, "Murderer, murderer, murderer."

"No," Daniel's father said and clapped his hands to his ears. "No!" He ran blindly through the woods. Branches stuck out into his path jabbing, scratching, and poking him. The ground itself became softer, giving way beneath his footfalls and grabbing at his boots. All the time the chant of "Murderer" followed him until he came to the wood's edge where it bordered the road. He stumbled out onto the pavement, weeping and dizzy. The air there was quiet. He curled up on the hot tarmac and convulsed with weeping until a car he didn't see came and took his life.

Long after the dogs had been called off and the searchers left without ever finding Daniel's body, a sapling grew near the base of the big oak. The old tree spoke to the sapling, "Is it everything you wanted?"

"Well," said the sapling, "I am small and weak."

"This is true," said the tree. "It is the secret nobody ever tells you about being a tree. First you must be small and weak and frail; if you can survive this, you can survive anything. In that way, I think being a tree is very much like being a man."

THE OPEN MOUTH

She's crying again.

My dream splits open to reveal my dark bedroom and a piercing wail that can only be Emily.

Let me guess, I think, it's three. I roll over and the clock confirms it. Three-oh-two to be exact. Hell, she's two minutes late.

I look over at my wife, sleeping peacefully, which is unusual. Any other night she'd already be awake, out of bed, making it easy for me to justify going back to sleep. Tonight, though, her chest rises and falls calmly, and her eyes remain shut. She gets so little sleep. I can't be selfish tonight.

I stumble-walk in the dark across the bedroom carpet and out into the hallway, navigating by memory. The wailing gets louder as I move closer to Emily's room.

She's going to hate this. When I get up to take care of her in the middle of the night, Emily does not shy away from announcing her displeasure. My wife feeds her to sleep. It takes longer, but Emily prefers it. I don't have that ability. When it's me who rocks her to sleep, she tries to get away. I have to hold her tight, grab her arms, keep her from slapping and flailing.

That works quicker. She goes to sleep when she resigns herself to the fact she can't move, but it's less pleasant overall.

There's the door, white, shining against the night's deep black. I pause to listen. She stops for a moment and hope rises in my chest. Sometimes she gives up. Sometimes nobody has to go in.

Another wail pierces the door. Dammit. I push it open too hard. Just go back to sleep, I beg wordlessly. The nightlight illuminates the room with a dim, blue glow. Emily stands in her crib. Shit. This is always harder when she's standing.

Emily sees me in the doorway and reacts as though a monster from her deepest nightmares entered the room. The wail becomes a cry of distress and intensifies.

No matter how many times I experience this, it's never easy. I choke the feeling down. This is not rejection. That's irrational. She's a baby. I clench my fists, let my fingernails bite into my palm, feel it sting. Deep breath out.

Emily scrambles, using the rail to walk around to the back of the crib, screaming at the wall, trying to get as far away from me as possible.

"Don't be such a fucking drama queen," I say under my breath, careful not to speak too loudly. My wife could hear that through the monitor. Dropping an F-bomb in the baby's room would be more trouble than it's worth, even though the baby has no idea what that means.

I cross the room in three steps, too aggressively. I grab Emily with both hands. Her screams are wild like a cornered animal. God dammit, I'm not going to hurt you. I hold her tight, restricting her arms and legs. Gotta get the message across. I rock her slowly left to right, bouncing gently. "Shh-shh-shh-shh."

She strains against me.

I tighten my hold.

Her face glows blue in the nightlight. She opens her mouth. Her eyes are closed. In this lack of light, her features are distorted. Her mouth expands, widens, her jaw drawing back like a snake trying to eat some rodent bigger than its head.

That's not right. I blink. I look up at the wall, at the door, the open closet. I look back at the baby.

The black hole of her mouth dominates her head. The black slits of her closed eyes are retreating up her forehead, back into the hairline.

It's a trick of the light. My arms are cold and the skin there gathers into gooseflesh. I squeeze her tighter against my bare chest as she heaves, trying to buck out of my hold. I close my eyes hard, try to blink away the hallucination brought on by too much dark, too little sleep.

When I look again, there are no eyes.

Her mouth is a round, wet, black hole that takes up the entire front of her head. Teeth are descending from the perfectly circular lipless edge like a leech or a lamprey. There are so many teeth, each one triangular, sharp.

No. I let go of my daughter, try to drop her, but she clings to me.

Her arms are too long, too strong. They wrap around me like a boa constrictor. She squeezes me tighter, wringing the breath from my chest. I try to push her away but her arms, like rubber, are locked around me, tied in a knot around my back.

I look down at her t-shirt and remember buying it at a store. My wife insisted on it. In big pink letters: *Daddy Makes Me Smile.*

Her head moves forward, her mouth suctioning to my bare chest, and the teeth sink in.

I scream and beat on her with my hands, but nothing changes. Why isn't my wife here? Hasn't she heard? The monitor is on and next to the bed but even if it weren't, we are loud, thrashing, screaming, thumping into walls, knocking over shelves.

The pain is intense.

Even though I can't see the blood she is drinking, I can feel it leaving my body in great slurping gulps. I'm lighter. My punches and wild swings are less effective. My stomach lurches and vomit boils in my throat. Dizziness hits and I blink. I fall to my knees, twisting, writhing. I blink again and I'm on my back. I feel blackout drunk. Am I going blind or is it darker?

The pressure on my chest loosens. I feel myself spill like a bucket tipped too far. The weight rolls off my chest and I let my head fall, roll in that direction so I can see her.

Emily's sitting up. Her clothes are dark, black. They weren't before, and I wonder if it's blood. My blood. I can't read her T-shirt anymore. Whatever happened to her face, her arms, they've retracted. Now she looks like my Emily. I smile in spite of myself, in spite of the fact I can taste blood, in spite of the floating feeling, encroaching blindness.

Emily tilts her head to the side and smiles back at me. "Daddy, don't be such a fucking drama queen," she says, dragging the syllables out like music.

Her first words.

YOU WILL BE THE ONE TO
FIND THIS

Timothy was not angry with his brother and sister when they left. He was now. Both Charlotte and Ben had left right after their mom's funeral. Neither said anything. Fair enough.

Timothy sat alone in the back corner of the home they all grew up in. He remembered it being tidy, but now it was stacked to the rafters with a lifetime's collected detritus.

The worst pile was in what his mother called her "craft room." But there was no evidence the space was used to produce any crafts. It was where his mother hoarded the most outlandish items in her collected mess. Bundles of herbs crumbled on the tables. Boxes of still-sandy seashells, stacks of old clothes and fabric scraps, tassels, baubles, marbles, loose change, books, bottles, jars, loomed over Timothy where he sat, right in the middle of it, crisscross applesauce, face buried in his hands.

The shoeboxes he piled around himself were each filled to overflowing with the kind of artifacts that were meaningless to everyone else and priceless—complicated—to him. One contained love letters his father wrote, each dated, starting about a year before his parents were married and ending a few days before his father died. Another box contained the pieces of the conch shell he and Ben knocked off the table when they were running around the house that same week. Some shards still had yellowed streaks of dried glue along the edges from when his mom tried to stick it together and gave up.

Timothy lifted his red face from his wet palms and picked up another box. His name was neatly printed on the lid. In smaller print below that, it said, *You will be the one to find this*.

Timothy grunted. A tear spilled from the corner of his eye then rolled hot down his cheek. God dammit. He ran his palm over the cardboard lid. This was heavier than the love notes but lighter than the conch. When he tilted it from side to side, something slid and clunked.

Timothy didn't want to open it. This was just like his mom. She always singled him out, saddled him with something, and every time she did, it always looked simple from a distance. Up close, it was always big, messy, and complicated. He looked at the boxes stacked in front of him, two high. He knew he was the only person to whom one was explicitly addressed because he was the responsible one. He was the one who cleaned up after whatever disaster. Death, flood, earthquake, deities descending from the sky to rain cleansing fire; good old Timothy would be here with the broom, the vacuum, the phone book full of contractors' numbers. So, she had left him this box.

He lifted the lid.

Timothy's hand trembled, so the empty mason jar danced on the box's flimsy floor. It was accompanied by a sealed envelope, nothing written on it.

Timothy laughed, a single loud bark of pure relief. This was like her to assign such importance to some meaningless thing. He put the box down, tore open the envelope, and pulled out the note.

This is me. All of me. Everything I am and everything I was at any moment is right here. Just think and listen.

What the hell did that mean? He looked from the note to

the jar, back to the letter. He thought about the conch and how he used to hold it to his ear so he could hear the ocean; it was just air flowing through the shell coupled with blood whooshing through the veins in his own head, but if he closed his eyes, he could smell the salt air.

He picked the jar up and uncapped it, then closed his eyes and covered his ear with the mouth. Inside the glass was an air-conditioner buzzing whoosh, not unlike the ocean but definitely not the ocean. He took a deep breath and stared at the bright red backs of his eyelids.

There were voices, children, distant, coming from down the hallway. Thumping footsteps ran heavy on hollow wood floors.

Timothy's eyes snapped open, and he gasped in the air. Just stress. Of course, he would hear things today. When was the last time he ate? He should go to the kitchen and get a snack.

He didn't.

Instead, he put the jar back to his ear. He closed his eyes again and listened. The whirring of the enclosed jar became an open window in a stiff breeze.

THE CURTAINS ARE BLOWING—THEIR SILKINESS ARCHES against his back, his neck. Irregular, clumsy children's footsteps chase each other through the house. He feels content. The boys are yelling, but not in anger. Their cries are distant, but he tries to focus, tries to make out what they are saying.

"By the power of Grayskull!"

That's Ben, age nine.

"Not so fast, He-Man!" Another boy cackles.

This is him, Timothy, thirty years ago. He is eleven.

He remembers this. Anxiety crawls up his spine. He wants to run from the room, yell at them to stop, but he can't.

He is vaguely aware of his body, still sitting on the worn wooden floor with the jar pressed against his ear.

But he also stands, walking lightly, in a way he has never walked before. He looks at his hands. They are not his. They do things without him, pulling sprigs from a bundle of dried herbs and tossing them into a stone mortar on the worktable. A wedding ring hugs his third finger, a bandage on his index. His nails are painted a pale pink. The knuckles are wrinkled, but the backs are smooth. He knows these hands.

His head swims from the smell of the herbs. He grabs the pestle and grinds. There are other things in the bowl, a red powder and a brownish liquid that turns the mixture into a slurry. He puts down the pestle and picks up a pair of rocks, flint. He smacks them together and scrapes first one spark, then another into the bowl. Smoke curls from the bowl and into the air. He clacks the two stones together faster, harder. One, two, three, four, five sparks. More smoke weaves upward. It turns colors. A single finger of flame emerges, first red, then green, then blue. The herbs crackle and the ingredients glom together into a single mass melted like candle wax.

A tubular body forms, black, the length of a toothpick. Legs emerge. Wings unfurl like ribbon, the same colors of the flame.

A butterfly stands in the mortar. It flaps its wings and lifts into the air toward the window to be carried off by the wind.

Timothy can't tell whose tears are streaming down his face—where his mother ends and he begins. There is perfection at this moment. The butterfly, the herb smell, the breeze and the gentle curtains, the sounds of the children playing at the front of the house—he should be afraid of what happens next. He can feel it coming in his bones, but his mother's happiness overwhelms his thoughts, and he falls back into it like a pile of fall leaves.

A shout sounds from the front of the house, a thud, a howling scrape of furniture being pushed across hardwood, then a crash.

No. The thought shrieks in Timothy's head, but not in his voice. Alarm quickly replaces concern, supplanted with the feeling of "surely not," but his feet move fast to the door. He's in the dark hallway, then the family room.

Sunlight streams through the open windows, and it's quiet like the air has been sucked out. The boys, one on the floor, sitting up, the other standing over him, paper-towel-roll sword still in hand. Both skinny, pale, freckled faces stare at Mom as though stunned. When she can hear something again, it is their breathing, both frightened and tired. Timothy doesn't want to see. The end table is at an odd angle, away from the corner between the wall and the couch, and it is empty. The same blow that knocked the table out of place unseated the conch from its stand and sent it rolling to the floor where it shattered.

"No," she says and raises a hand to her head.

"Mom," Ben says, standing perfectly still, having dropped his cardboard sword and now holding both palms out to her in a "stop, slow down" gesture. "Mom, I'm sorry. It just—"

Panic rises in her chest. A sick feeling works its way into her. *This was holding everything together.*

HE IS SOMEWHERE DIFFERENT. IT IS A LONG TIME AGO. Timothy can tell because when he looks at his hands, his mother's hands, the knuckles are not wrinkled. This is before there was a family. His mother and father are falling in love. It's in the way his mother feels light, and his father heavy, like she's falling into him, giving in to a happy gravity.

They're in a store—the kind of cheesy souvenir shop that haunts every corner in a beach town. Plastic baskets filled with shark's teeth and seashells line the hastily built wooden displays. There are colossal wicker baskets of die-cast pirate doubloons, racks of sunglasses. Timothy's mother and father just walked in off the beach. They don't even have shoes on—every step his mother takes grinds sand into her soles.

A younger version of his father, less fat, more muscle, faces some shelves along the wall. He wears blue swim trunks and nothing else. Mom approaches him and wraps her hands around his shoulders, buries her fingers in his chest hair. Timothy grimaces. She leans into him, putting her chin on his shoulder. In doing so, she notices the conch on a high shelf above the smaller shells. It's pink and swirled with white like cupcake icing.

"It's basically snail vomit," his father says.

"What?"

"Snail vomit," he says. His grin screams mischief. "Conch isn't the shell's name. It's the name of the snail. They ingest a whole bunch of sea salt and minerals and stuff and excrete it like a paste to make shells for themselves."

She slaps him playfully in the shoulder. "It's beautiful," she says.

"It's also a hundred and fifty bucks."

"I know."

They don't have much money left. They only saved so much for their trip, and they'll be going back tomorrow to peanut butter sandwiches and ramen noodles until he gets paid in two weeks. She unwraps her arms from around his shoulders and steps back.

He probably thinks she's stupid for wanting it, but she loves that it looks sweet like hard candy. She hopes she isn't moping. It isn't about the shell. She's tired of waiting on paychecks, eating stale bread, making every penny stretch until she feels like she will snap. The store suddenly feels claustrophobic. She feels like she did when she was a child, and her father would scold her, spank her for asking for things. She couldn't help it. Children want things; that's not her fault, and it isn't her fault right now, either.

Damn him for shutting her down like that, for pretending like her wants didn't deserve any more than a one-sentence rebuke, and then walking off silently to look at the next rack of cheap junk without a word. She knows it isn't his fault either and that she is acting like a child. She is grateful she has refrained from saying any of this out loud. They're now on separate aisles.

Air. I need air.

Outside is better. It's hot even though the sun is down. She can hear the gulls finishing up their hunt. The waves shush across the boardwalk, beyond the sand. She slides her butt down the shop window and sits on the sidewalk. With her head in her hands, she gulps salt air.

Better.

The bell rings above the shop door. He steps out, carrying a bag, and sits down next to her. She can smell his sunscreen and the Marlboro Reds he smokes. She doesn't look at him right away.

Stop acting like a child, she hears, but he doesn't say that. He lights another cigarette, takes a drag, then exhales. The smoke cloud floats past, and she knows then that it will kill him. The realization hits her like a truck. With all the certainty in the world, she sees him dying, gasping for breath, a clot of cancer as big as a baseball in his lungs.

He places a hand on her knee. "Okay?" he asks.

"Yeah."

"I know what it's like," he says.

"What?"

"I know what it's like to need space," he says. "To, I don't know, freak out, I guess?"

She doesn't say anything.

"I don't know what's going on in your head, and it's okay. I'll be here when you're done," he says. "I'll always be here when you're done."

He is staring forward toward the ocean. The cigarette hovers right in front of his face, supported by two fingers on his right hand. His left arm is hugging his knees where he has them pulled up in front of him just like her. She looks down at the bag in between them. It holds a parcel wrapped in tan paper, the size of a football. She peels back a corner and sees a pink and white swirl.

"It's just snail vomit," he says.

She takes his hand from around his knees, raises it to her lips, and kisses it's rough back, below the knuckles. Then she lays her head on his shoulder. "Ass," she says.

They both smile and stare out at the sea.

IT IS LATER.

What are we going to do without him? He's holding everything together.

Timothy looks down at his mother's shaking hands. He doesn't want to be here. He knows what this is. His pulse quickens, and his vision wavers.

He calms himself. This is important. He has to stay.

He's dying, his mother thinks.

They're in the hospital. Complicated, noisy, horrible equipment made of screens, knobs, and gray plastic are stacked next to the bed where his father lays unconscious, not asleep because she could feel him if he was sleeping. She can only feel that damned thing in his chest, strangling him.

I didn't think it'd be this soon. I would have prepared.

The doctor said it was about the size of a baseball.

He was tired a lot. That was the first sign. Then he coughed. It was already too late to do much. He was playing with Charlotte the first time he coughed up blood. They sat on the couch in the living room, bouncing up and down. Charlotte laughed in the way she only laughed with him, free but private. The cough sounded wet like they all did, but he stopped and put the baby down on the couch beside him, her pink onesie splattered with red. So were his lips.

It was the emergency room first, then a few doctors, first

their general, and then a specialist. It was the specialist who finally told them what his wife already knew.

It's been a month. At first he was tired but holding. Now he has a malignant, throbbing mass in his chest, and he needs a machine to breathe. There wasn't even time for chemotherapy to latch on. They didn't get to fight it.

She knows what she has to do. It's going to hurt.

SHE STANDS IN THE CRAFT ROOM, DIM RED LIGHT THROUGH the curtains her only illumination. Boxes and baskets and piles of papers and books and rolls of cloth are spread out on the table.

It has to be something fragile, she thinks, and something meaningful. Something I can keep out so he sees it every day, so it will hold.

The shell. She takes the conch down from its shelf.

Her mother used to call this magic, but she despises the term. It's not magic. It's negotiation, like haggling with a drug dealer. Small stuff, parlor tricks, make a penny disappear, pull a rabbit out of a hat, doesn't cost much at all: a pinprick, a few drops. But the important stuff costs more. If you want to unseat reality from its predetermined track, you have to do it by force. When you have no strength, no currency left, it falls back into the groove. This will kill her if it goes on long enough. She will live for them both and probably burn out twice as fast, but they will live long enough to see the kids grow. They will only miss the painful end full of aches and disease.

Excuses.

Damn this thing. Given more time, she could have found a better way.

Herbs first, crumbled into the conch. Now the water that is not water. She reaches for the jar, and when she touches the glass with her fingertip, it glows blue. This liquid is valuable, impossible. She pours it all in. Too much? There is no time for half measures. Now the knife, the blood. She grips the knife's wooden handle in her right hand and, as she has only seen done in movies, grips the smooth, narrow, cold blade in her left. She closes her eyes tight and drags the edge over her palm.

She has heard that the mind blocks the pain and only reveals it after the adrenaline has worn off, but this she feels immediately. She bites down to keep from screaming, and her throat releases a whimper. She cuts deeply so the blood will flow. Tiny imperfections in the blade grab and snag her flesh in the cut. She wraps her wounded hand into a fist and watches the bright red blood pour into the conch. The more blood, the more impenetrable the pact. She squeezes harder. More. She feels light like her mind is floating. Too much. She grabs blindly for the shelf at eye level, finds a wad of cloth, and wraps it around her hand. Her teeth grind.

Now the hair—his hair. This is easy, nearly an afterthought. The pact needs something to latch onto. She drops it in, picks up the conch, and mixes it. The pink-white swirl on the outside of the shell curves over and envelops the glowing gore inside as if it knows it harbors something terrible, delicate, wildly important.

She feels it—something has cast a line and hooked onto her soul. It's a single gossamer thread now, but it will grow. As they age, more lines will be cast, and they will find more purchase in her, pull her down. She will age more quickly, feel worse, and be sicker. Right now, she feels like she could use a cup of coffee.

She welcomes the thread because he is on the other end.

She is frantic.

The protection charm didn't work. Or it did, and this was when it was supposed to happen. Or it wasn't strong enough. Or she wasn't.

She is in the family room.

"I'm sorry, Mom," Ben says. He cries, panicked, because she is, too.

She cannot pay attention to him right now. He will survive. She crawls on her knees next to the upset table, collecting the pink-white swirled shards, picking splinters out of the seams between the boards in the wood floor.

Little Timothy crawls toward her from where he landed on his butt a couple feet away. He looks at her with a face streaked with dirt and tears and tries to help. He picks up a piece, and she snatches it from his hand. Its sharp edge cuts his finger.

"No! Don't touch it!" she screams and pushes his shoulder with her palm.

He falls back onto his rear. He doesn't say anything, just stares. He doesn't understand.

Neither of them understands. Neither knows what they've done. And they won't. Not yet. It would not be fair to burden them with this. They are only children.

For the first time in their lives, she hates them.

A sob escapes her lips. She takes the gathered pieces and clutches them to her chest, stands, and runs down the hallway to the craft room door. She slams it behind her. An empty mason jar falls off its shelf. She picks it up and rights it, meticulously placing it on its side with the opening facing out into the middle of the room. So many important things are fragile.

The glue doesn't work. She knew it wouldn't. She sits on the floor to sob until he comes home. She hopes he will come home.

His heavy, booted feet step into the house. He adds weight to the air. The boys have been afraid to come in to check on her. They are terrified about the shell, about what they have done. She hears them chattering, hushed, and she can see him tousle their hair, one with each hand. He winks at Charlotte where she stands peeking from around the corner at the end of the hallway. He tells them to wait outside. He will go in and check on Mom.

She buries her head in her knees. He takes his cue, and walks softly over to sit on the floor next to her. He pulls out his pack of

Marlboros. Lights, now. Too little, too late. He lights the smoke and draws it in deeply, coughing. She recognizes the sound, and knows the cancer is back, stronger this time—stronger than her. Things are falling back into the track. She held it back for as long as she could.

"The threads are breaking," she says. She counted them as they snapped all afternoon.

"I don't know what that means," he says, "But, I imagine it has something to do with . . ." He trails off, not sure how to finish.

"I can't stop them," she says. "They were holding everything together."

He puts a hand on her knee. "Maybe it's time they let go."

"No," she says.

"Maybe."

They sit without talking. She cries into her knees. He smokes his cigarette.

"Was I supposed to die?" he asks.

She looks at him. He's pale, and sweat shimmers on his forehead. His eyes look sunken with black circles.

"Ellie, answer me."

"Yes," she says.

"You've been different," he says. "Ever since I was in the hospital, you've been different."

"Yes."

"I have, too, though," he says.

She nods.

"I felt like I couldn't stand on my own. How the hell do I describe that? Tenuous. It felt tenuous. Like being propped up by a rotting board," he says. He isn't talking to her. He's talking to himself, to the floor, like she isn't there next to him. He furrows his brow.

"I wanted to give you—to give *us* time," she says.

"Time," he repeats absently. "How much does time cost?"

"You can only buy it with more time."

He looks at the conch on the floor below the table. Her precious blood is dried in a ring that says it was too deep, that she gave too much. He understands. It was her propping him up. She'd been tired and distant of late, and he worried he did something wrong, but that wasn't it.

"You didn't need to do that," he says.

"I would have."

"I know, but I'm glad you don't have to anymore. We're both free now."

She lays her head on his shoulder and leans into him, giving in to that old happy gravity.

He coughs and there's red on his lips.

LAST TIME TIMOTHY SAW THROUGH HIS OWN EYES, THERE WAS sunlight coming into the room through the red curtains. Now it was dark. The only light source was the little lamp on the table that was on before Timothy sat on the floor.

Timothy thought about an article he read some time ago about how dust is made up mostly of dead skin. He thought about the pieces of his mother that were still there. How much of her was embedded in the walls, the cracks in the floor? They would never be able to extract her fully from this room. In the graveyard, she was dead, decaying, melting into the earth, but she'd been dying here for years, little pieces sloughing off and floating to rest among the junk.

He took the jar away from his ear. Holding it there for hours had made him sweat, and the hair around his temple was damp. His arm cramped as he unfolded it, stretched it with the jar still in his hand. He felt as if he had metastasized into his spot on the floor. He wasn't sure he could get up if he tried. The skin on his face was stiff where tears had dried.

Timothy sat the jar down and stared at it. He picked up the

note from his mother again and let his eyes follow her pen strokes. *This is me*, it said. *All of me.*

He understood it now—she was wrong. It wasn't her; it was a picture. It was a fantastic picture that saw and heard and acted and explained and thought, but it couldn't do those things in a new way. It would never laugh or write a note, never make life or console it. It only repeated.

He looked to the box that contained his father's letters. It once held a pair of his father's work boots. Timothy remembered the sound of those boots on the floor, each footfall a massive doubled clomp that conveyed weight, always on its way to something, never away.

He flicked the box open and picked up the papers his mother had carefully laid flat, straightening out the folds and wrinkles in an attempt to preserve them. The oldest were yellow, stiff with age. Some were beginning to fall apart at the creases. These old ones said things like *your scent drives me mad* and quoted song lyrics—something that seemed deep and thoughtful when you were young but aged poorly. The newer ones were less fragile like his father's pen just left the page and might return at any moment.

One page stayed at the bottom of the box. It was smaller than the others. He picked it up and turned it over—hospital stationery. This was the last one.

Ellie, it said, *thank you for loving me enough to try.*

Anger crawled into Timothy's chest. He wanted the letter to be longer. He wanted a revelation, an apology, at least a mention in his father's last written thoughts. Most of all, he wished for absolution. He wouldn't get it. He wanted to be told, unequivocally, that none of this was his fault, or Ben's fault, or even Charlotte's who had done nothing. He wanted to know that he played no part in this, or if he had, at least to be forgiven. He had known since he was eleven years old, sitting on the family room floor watching his mother panic over the shards of a pink and white seashell, that he had done something more than making a boy's mistake. Since the moment he stood in a hospital room next to his mother, who was holding Charlotte in her lap, and they watched his father's chest stop moving, he had known that was, at least in part, his fault. His and Ben's.

If they had been a little more careful, his father might have lived longer, might have seen him graduate high school, seen him get married, been there to talk him through his divorce. He wanted someone to tell him he was wrong, that the man would have died anyway, that it was his father's fault for smoking all those damned cigarettes.

None of this would have happened. Life doesn't end that clean. His father couldn't tie up all the loose ends.

But there was something Timothy could do. He could break the jar.

He'd do it on the driveway, throw it down, hear the glass explode as the magic turned into so much trash. He would get the broom, sweep the shards into his mother's dustpan, and forget about all this. He was good at making himself forget.

But he didn't *want* to forget.

Knowledge is sometimes painful, but the pain is how you learn. This was an opportunity to see himself, his father, his brother, his sister through one of the only pairs of eyes that ever mattered, to do more than see. To understand. Know all truths.

Maybe he was thinking of this all wrong. The jar wasn't a picture, wasn't an imperfect stand-in, a mistake. *Everything I am and everything I was at any moment are here*, the note said. The jar was a letter—his mother's last. Perhaps he had only read part of it.

Moreover, maybe he had asked the wrong questions. Every human being, parents most of all, are made of complexity. They are all crisscrossing interweaving thoughts, feelings, actions, regrets, triumphs, pride, and shame, and there was no reason why what he had seen had to be the final word. Maybe this fantastic letter could *cure* everything.

Something let go inside him. He was not the center of this or any other universe. Maybe she had more to tell him. That's why this was left for him, she knew he would be the one to find it. Because he'd know what to do with it.

"Just think and listen," his mother said.

That is precisely what he would do.

AND THE REVEL WENT
WHIRLINGLY ON

The stranger spoke for the first time that night, "Beginnings are always preceded by endings. Renewal by destruction, rebirth by violent death." His voice was a little more than a gargling choke, only audible because everyone at the long, luxuriously appointed dining table was suddenly, silently holding their breath.

Miranda was the first to break the awestruck quiet. This was her house, after all. She spoke around a hunk of partially chewed meat, "Who are you? You have sat at my table all evening not speaking and this is the first you say?"

"No, no, Miranda, this young man has a point," said Nathan Chalmers, spreading his arms wide and flashing an arrogant grin. "In a few months, when the plague dies down and the dregs are all dead and can't spread the thing, it will be up to us to renew society. We were chosen for a reason!"

Other heads bobbed up and down in agreement. Voices murmured ascent.

"You survive only," said the stranger from behind his mask, "because of your money."

"Sir," said Colonel Hottenroth, a huge man with a Viginian drawl and a walrus mustache. His own mask was askew because he kept pulling it aside to shovel food underneath, some of which hung in filthy ropes down his chin. "Certainly you understand basic economics?"

An uncomfortable chuckle sounded from all around the table. "Everyone here has obtained their wealth by the sweat of their brow. We have prospered because we are stronger, smarter, and more diligent. We used our wealth to filter the air and make our homes safe. As have you, if you are at this table with us tonight. Which, clearly, you *are*. Be glad, son! Society chose us to survive long before it knew there was a choice to be made!" He raised his glass, slopping white wine over the side.

Others followed suit, raising their glasses, laughing and murmuring to each other in agreement.

Miranda squinted at the stranger. There was something familiar about his voice, the way it gargled and popped. She thought of her husband, that weak little weasel of a man, standing on their porch screaming at her through the living room window. He swore the clean, filtered air inside the house would drive the infection from his blood even as his skin boiled and tore in bloody lesions. She left him there, screaming until he died twitching and melting on the porch.

His voice sounded very much like the stranger's.

"Do we know you? Who did you come with?" Surely he was not infected. The Clean System would have sounded an alarm. Her heart raced just the same.

"You do not know me," the stranger said. "But you will. We should have met long ago." The stranger shot his bloodshot eyes over to the Colonel. "You say you are chosen, that you will be the one to renew your race, but the renewal to come has nothing to do with you. Our Mother has realized her mistake. The world will be reborn without you." The stranger stood, sending his chair screeching backward. "You survived this long because you are cowards. I will remedy this." The stranger pulled off his mask. Beneath his hood, skin boiled and crawled. Gaping lesions dripped with dark fluid.

"Christ!" Chewed meat dropped from Miranda's mouth. "You're infected."

"How did the Clean System not catch him?" a woman at the other end of the table screamed.

"I am not *infected*," the stranger said. "I *am* infection." He spread his arms wide and his flesh melted into the air. His tattered clothing slowly folded in on itself, settling in a heap on the floor.

The Clean System blared its alarm. Too late.

Miranda's skin sizzled. A sore opened on her arm and popped like a bubble spraying infected mucous on the tablecloth. She opened her mouth to scream but all that came out was a wet moan.

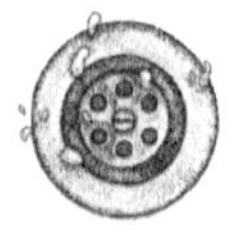

DRAIN

When James was eight years old, a spider crawled out of the drain and up his leg while he was in the shower. It was a big one, black with yellow stripes. Little hairs sunk into his skin with each rapid footstep, stinging as it sprinted up his shin.

Twenty years later, that's the first thing James thinks of when he feels the tickling sensation on his toe. The water from the shower batters his head, falls in sheets over his closed eyes, and fills his nostrils. He is left only with his sense of touch. His brain delights in torturing him with the memory of the spider. He breathes in water and bitter shampoo. His hands shoot to his face to squeegee the wet away and free his senses.

The second thing James thinks of is the embarrassment he felt all those years ago. The spider scrambled up his leg and headed for his crotch, which had only just become something he cared about. Adrenaline flooded every gland and receptor it could find. James slapped the spider off his knee with an awkward sideways karate chop that sent the creature *thunking* into the shower tile. He screamed as high and as loud as his vocal cords allowed then bounded through the shower curtain, through the house, into the living room where his parents and three older brothers sat playing Monopoly. He stood, naked, wet, and panting, as they laughed.

So, now, in the shower, with something tickling his big toe and a face full of soap, he uses all the shame from his childhood to shove down his panic, and move his foot. He turns his face toward the shower jet to clear away the soap, steps out of the water, wipes it away, and opens his eyes. His vision is bleary, so when he looks at the floor he can't tell what's sticking out of the drain.

His vision clears. A shock of black *hair* protrudes from a single square grate in the drain cover, defiantly holding its place against the torrent heading for the pipes.

The miserable bitch has been dead for months and I am still dealing with her mess, he hisses silently in his mind, a frown marring his face.

His wife, Kathryn, was a neat person in most respects, except for the hair. All married couples find things to fight about. For some, it becomes a sport. James could always count on another round of "the hair in the god-damned drain" she'd left in clumps every single time she showered. James always showered before Kathryn, so the hair moldered in the grate for twenty-four hours by the time James saw it. He'd have to pick up the nasty tangles and feel the cold damp of it as he carried it to the toilet and flushed it. It was a pre-shower ritual: scoop up the clump, flush it, gag, get in the shower.

This was not the only thing they fought about. In fact, the thing that finally made him put a bullet in her skull while she slept was the snoring. She sounded like she was tickling a pig in their bed every night. He'd tried earplugs, headphones, even sleeping on the couch, but in the end it was more than he could handle.

James has slept great ever since he dropped her in the river, pinned to the bottom with ropes and cinder blocks. He sleeps like a baby.

There must be miles of hair down there, he thinks, staring

down at the clump. He makes a mental note to call a plumber as soon as he gets out of the shower. For now, though, he uses his big toe to kick the clump back into the drain where the water does its job and carries it out of sight. James takes a deep breath and steps back into the shower stream face first.

As soon as the water hits him, closing his eyes, flowing backward up his nose, he feels the tickle again. This time, it's on his ankle. He jerks his foot up and pivots, landing against the cold tile. The hair lays limp, curled on the plastic floor, extending from the drain as though telling itself to act natural.

Fuck this. I'll shower tomorrow after the plumber comes. He pushes the shower stall open, steps out with his left foot and —*thump*. His right foot jerks back down. An old familiar panic wells up in his chest, the same feeling from when he was eight with that spider. He whips his head around and looks at his foot. The hair, much longer now, lays across his foot, curling around his ankle like a taunt. James lets out an ugly laugh full of panic and mock. That didn't happen, and you're an idiot for thinking it did.

He picks his foot up to proceed as planned, refusing to look at the insignificant clump of old trash. *Thunk*. Again. This time, James screams. No. Stupid. No. He lifts the foot again, but this time it is held fast to the floor. The hair coils around his ankle, digging in like rope, pulling taut between his ankle and the drain.

He dives forward. The hair holds and James falls, naked and wet, onto the cold ceramic tile. Pain flares in his ankle. He grits his teeth and tries to drag himself forward, pulling against the hair with his ruined ankle, already purple and swollen. He makes no progress. He stops, gives up, face down on the tile, and sobs.

A wet slap sounds behind him on the shower stall floor. No. Don't look at it. He rolls his body onto his side so he can crane his neck around. The metal drain grate pops off and flips to the side of the hole, spinning like a coin. Another wet slap. There are more hair tendrils arcing out of the drain, bent like elbows, slapping their ends like hands onto the plastic. Eight hair-arms, thick as sapling trees, brace against the plastic all around the drain and flex. Sucking, grunting sounds are emitted as *it* drags itself up through the pipe using the hair like a corkscrew's wings.

James's ragged breath comes through in shallow bursts. He shakes, cold and afraid on the tile, and pulls against the hair. His swollen ankle shoots bolts of pain up his thigh and into his groin. He screams and grits his teeth as tears mingle with the water on his face.

A mottled gray, cylindrical tube of rotting flesh emerges from the drain—canned salmon, only there isn't a smidgen of pink. The mess slides its way out of the hole, one crackling, undulating pull at a time.

It's long. First inches and then feet squeeze up from below until it towers, wobbling over him. The column nearly touches the nine foot ceiling. All of it is out of the drain now and the tower collapses onto the floor in a succession of rapid, hollow thumps, then lays squirming in a grotesque pile.

A crackling popcorn sound emerges from the gray mass. Shattered bones snap back into place, reassembling themselves into the remains of a person.

The smell strikes him, and James's gut boils. It's a mix of sulphureous, sun-spoiled meat and rotting fish that hangs in his nostrils, clings to his skin. Gray flesh slapped haphazardly against bone and cartilage. Remnants of pink, rotted muscle, split over the knees and at the shoulders so the meat can shine through, white in places, like flaking catfish. Its black hair hangs shoulder-length and its breasts droop. Its stomach is swollen, and something moves inside.

When it raises its face, James is not surprised to see it's Kathryn. Her blind eyes are stark white in her face and her teeth blackened, yellow-orange drool dripping from her sagging, gray lips.

Oh god, her stomach. How long has it been, how many months? James renews his effort to scramble backward, crab-walking on his hands and feet. The hair holds. The wet floor tile is a treadmill going the wrong direction. She wasn't pregnant, oh, no, no, no. Piss flows down James's leg and splashes onto the floor.

Kathryn raises her white-blind eyes to his. Her ruined mouth splits open in a grin that sends more orange fluid spurting onto her chest and dribbling down onto the beige plastic shower floor. The thing inside her presses against her distended belly. There is a hand, a foot, a face, as it roils inside. The face stops and the mouth opens and closes, splitting the belly skin. Kathryn only laughs—a sound made of mucous and fluid, a rhythmic boiling of gore in her throat.

The child that emerges from Kathryn chews through her midsection with a full set of sparkling white serrated shark's teeth that fill its mouth so fully it can't close its lips. It flops onto the shower floor on its back then throws itself onto all fours. Its skin is as gray as its mother's and its arms and legs and tummy are globular fat rolls that would be cute on another baby. A penis protrudes from between its legs.

Is this my son?

Kathryn smiles as she reaches down and yanks the umbilical cord in two. The phlegm boils in Kathryn's throat and she mouths the words, *go to daddy*.

The baby-thing's hand slaps on the shower floor as it crawls forward. It clears the shower and flops across the tile between James's legs. He tries to kick it away, but cannot bend his leg enough. He sits up and swings at it with his palm, trying to swat it away like he did the spider all those years ago. Unlike that unfortunate arachnid, this creature clings to the floor. It brushes against his inner thigh below his crotch and where it touches, it bites.

A sizable piece of his flesh tears free. Blood pours out of the hole like a broken water balloon. James screams and swings his hands at the thing to no effect. The child smacks when it chews, slurping the mix of red blood and viscous black saliva back into it's mouth between bites. Bone is visible through the meat of James's leg as the baby works its way upward.

The pain is gone and James is on his back again. Numbness washes over him. He stares at the white ceiling. Dark creeps in around the edges of his vision. His wife croaks with fluid laughter. His son makes happy little moans as he eats.

His son.

She never said she was pregnant. Did she even know? How many months has it been? Nine. It's been nine months. He deserves this. Son. A growing boy. He would laugh if he could.

Darkness. Smacking. Gorging. Pressure. Nothing. Nothing. Thank god, it's nothing.

THE BLACK WOOD

Merek stood at the line between sunlight and shadow. Behind him was his home, the ancient stone longhouse that had sheltered his forefathers for centuries. Before him stood the writhing wall of black trees that took his son.

In the nightmares, Merek nursed a cup of hot broth on the great wooden porch. The sun peered over the horizon as Rowan played in the yard between the house and trees. Even through the baby fat that still clung to his cheeks, Merek could see the man his son would grow into. Merek cherished these moments around the glorious dawn when things were quiet.

The sole occupants of his ancestors' ancient dwelling, he and Rowan rose early to tend to domestic tasks, including harvesting wheat in the field behind the house.

A whisper rose up around them like the rustling of leaves, "Rowan."

The boy heard. Merek heard too and looked up from his thoughts. Rowan stopped playing with the wooden horse Merek had carved for him and stood, putting the horse in the trouser pocket and raising his face to the air, listening. Merek rose, too.

"Rowan."

They both turned toward the forest where the whisper came.

The trees moved, jerky and mechanical at first, but gaining grace. Their bark liquefied and pooled until the massive trunks turned black and viscous. Swaying branches created a hypnotic rhythm, arresting Merek's attention for one—or several —moments.

As Merek shook off the enchantment, Rowan charged toward the tree line. His son laughed and ran, waving his small hands in the air as he neared. The strange liquid trees bent down, reaching with bare branches to gather up the boy. Merek sprinted to the scene with all his strength—not fast enough. Tree limbs embraced Rowan, hiding him from sight, and then scooped. By the time Merek reached the forest's edge, he was breathless and screaming, but the trees were once again just trees, rough bark and still, tangled limbs.

His boy was gone.

Was it only a dream? Merek's father told him never to enter the wood, and Merek listened, even though his father never said why. Now he knew—the forest was alive. Every day since Rowan was taken, Merek stepped into the tree line only to find himself stepping out through his own front door, the trees still across the lawn, his boy still gone.

They will not deny me entry again.

He wrenched his sword's hilt, thinking of the old man in the village who'd told him all the secrets his father had not. There was a reason his ancestral home was built at the edge of this stain upon the earth. Merek had dug up the sword from the cold earth beneath its foundation. His father had denied this weapon, hidden it away. Merek would not. And when he brought Rowan home, he would train him, then pass the sword to his son, as it should be.

Merek stepped into the shadow of trees, a chill deep in his

bones. This time, as he crossed the threshold into the forest, it did not turn him back but recoiled. The sword vibrated in his white-knuckled hand as he neared. This was its purpose. Again he remembered the old man's words, "It is a key, not a sword." Perhaps it was both.

Though it was noon, only a dull, gray glow emanated from the trees themselves. The canopy swayed and swirled as if it were an otherworldly ceiling of a great hall. The tree trunks were closely spaced columns, and the fallen leaves a thick, deep carpet. No sound broke through these woods, not birdsong, nor animal cries. Merek's footsteps fell muffled and dead on his ears, and even that faint noise seemed a violation of some sacred crypt. Frigid air burned the skin on his forehead and cheeks while moldering rot odors ringed his nostrils.

Merek walked deeper in, and whispered voices broke the quiet, rising from the forest floor in a myriad of splashing raindrops. Thousands of them, all unintelligible save one.

"Merek."

The same hushed voice that had called for Rowan.

Merek responded by tightening his grip on the sword, the vibrations from it like the sun's warmth in his palm. Tree bark around him once again turned smooth, liquid. The trunks bowed and wavered in time as if to an unholy music none could hear but them.

Merek closed his eyes.

"You do not need that sword. Just leave it," voices rose in cacophonous agreement.

For a moment he felt the full weight of his task, pure, dark, hopeless. I can't do this. Merek visualized the sword falling from his hands. He thought of turning and running back home. He thought of the tiny, empty bed across the room from his own. *Rowan.*

Something sharp scratched Merek's arm, and he opened his eyes. The trees leaned toward him, extending their whiplike limbs but guarded as if unsure of his intentions. He raised the sword above his head.

"Let me pass!" The sword pulsed against his palm. A yellow light shone from above, from the white jewel in the hilt.

The trees recoiled and stood at attention, but one lingered. Its trunk was bigger and thicker than the rest. It must be older.

It leaned down, probing with its limbs. A blood droplet clung to the sharpened tip of one limb. This was the limb that had scratched him. Perhaps it had gathered a taste for him.

Merek's stomach turned. He sliced the sword down in an arc, severing the limb. It dropped to the ground and lay still, a common stick. A high-pitched animal squeal split the air and the tree backed away. Waves and ripples shot through the trunk's liquid surface.

Merek ran. What manner of forest was this where trees could hunt men? His heart raced. Was it possible for Rowan to have survived this place for three days on his own? Merek stopped and fell to the bleak, leaf-carpeted ground. First to his knees, and then down onto his side. His chest shuddered with each deep, wheezing breath. The scratch on his forearm ached like a much larger wound. Weakness seized him. It seemed as though poison coursed through him, pulsing from the cut. He refused to look at it. "Please, God, let me live long enough to find my boy. Then the forest can have me."

His vision faded and all went black.

The day after Rowan's disappearance into the Black Wood, Merek went to see the old man called Gwyddion. The thought of it repulsed him. He would not normally consider it, but the old man was rumored to have arcane knowledge, and Merek was out of his depth.

He knocked. The door opened and he entered.

The old man lived in a one room cabin outside the village.

Every surface was piled with jars, dried husks of dead creatures, and odd machines Merek could not pretend to understand. Earthy brown hues colored the interior except for the fire that blazed in the stone hearth against one wall. The flames glowed green around the edges and cast an emerald light into the room that made the old man's face appear cadaverous.

Gwyddion stood hunching to keep from hitting his head on the thatched roof. Merek gasped and stepped back. The old man smelled of sweat and burning coals. A long, tattered cloak was draped over his angular frame and dragged over the floor, pooling at his feet. The old man looked at Merek, an idly curious expression on his face.

"I am Merek—"

"Son of Carac, father of Rowan," the old man said as if he had heard all this before. His voice was high and clear. A skeletal hand escaped his cloak, index finger extended. He waved it in a circular motion as his half-lidded eyes rolled upward. "Yes, yes, I know who you are."

"Then you must also know why I am here."

"Yes," the old man's voice lowered to a deep rumble.

"My son."

"Yes, it seems poor Rowan was *stupid* enough to heed the Black Wood's call."

"You will not speak of my boy that way!"

Gwyddion turned back to the fire and stooped. His body seemed to shrink. He grabbed the iron poker from the hearth and jabbed at the logs. "I have known this day would come," the old man said, unaffected by Merek's tone. "I have known it ever since Carac abandoned the old ways. When fathers hide the truth from their sons, the world does not forget."

"What truth? What old ways?"

"You are *more* than a farmer, Merek son of Carac. The wheat behind your house is not your chief concern, nor was it your father's. Do you know how long your family has lived in the house at the edge of the Black Wood?"

Merek thought. His father never spoke of such things. "I do not."

"Neither do I," said the old man, raising an eyebrow, "and I am very old indeed. But ask yourself. Why would anyone build a house so close to that cursed, haunted place?"

Merek felt his gut roil. He and Carac never saw eye to eye. His father rarely spoke more than three words at a time, and they were rarely about anything other than the wheat or some other chore. Was it his father's fault Rowan was taken?

"Your line has long stood between the people of this village and the forest. It was your grandfather's duty, as well as your father's, and it has been passed to you, though you did not know it. Your father rejected this truth, did not think he or his progeny should have to be responsible for such a burden. The wood moves slow. It creeps and sniffs and shows wild patience, but it sees now that you are unprotected, that the guardian line has fallen into disrepair. It has struck first so the war might be born anew. If you do not meet its challenge, we shall be overrun."

Merek stared at the old man with his mouth agape but said nothing. His heart raced.

"Go now, Merek, son of Carac, father of Rowan." The old man again faced Merek and stood to his full, unnatural height. "Pull up the floorboards of your house. You will know the spot when you stand upon it. Dig into the earth to find the weapon your father never wanted you to have. Go into the Black Wood and find your son. Show the forest that the guardian lives. If you do not, you doom us all."

MEREK WOKE FROM A DREAM HE DID NOT REMEMBER. HE WAS not at home. Leaves crunched beneath him. He was still in the forest. Something else was there, too. It snuffled and rustled. A cool wetness pressed against his cheek.

Wolves.

He remembered where the sword fell when he'd collapsed and he groped for it. Half covered in leaves, he closed his fist around the leather-wrapped handle. It pulsed in his hand. Merek leaped to his feet, striking in the direction of the panting thing's noises. The sword's tip found purchase and dug through flesh.

Before him stood a gigantic black dog, wet and sleek. At the end of its neck, where a dog's head should have been, sat a gore-caked human skull, its eye sockets empty except for an unnatural yellow light, mouth crammed with canine fangs. A thick, gray, human tongue lolled from its mouth. Its wounded shoulder bubbled and smoked from the cut. It unhinged its jaw and from deep in its throat issued the scream of a human baby.

Merek screamed too and leaped backward, but the beast retreated and ran behind a tree.

The scratch on Merek's forearm throbbed. He looked at it. The swollen flesh had turned black and green, oozing dark liquid that was almost like blood in the dim light, but Merek knew better.

What now? The old man told him of his role, told him of the sword, but the Black Wood was vast, much larger than it seemed from the outside. He had no idea where to begin looking for his son. His arm hurt. The poison from the wound continued spreading through him, making him sluggish. The dog-thing shook leaves behind a tree trunk. What other horrible abominations awaited him in this place?

The rustling grew louder. Merek squinted at the hundreds of slick, black columnar trunks surrounding him like rows of soldiers.

From behind each trunk, stepped one of the dog-things. They squared their shoulders, hundreds in perfect phalanx. Each of their dripping, skeletal jaws dropped open and the din of a thousand infants wailing threatened to drive the sanity from Merek's mind.

As the first creature attacked, he fell on his rear and the palm of his left hand, his right still holding the vibrating sword.

The beast landed hard on his chest, pushing him down, and screamed into his face. Merek swung the sword at its neck. Its cry was silenced as the skull fell to Merek's chest with a lifeless *thunk* and then rolled to the forest floor. The creature's body remained where it was for a moment, as if unaware of its head's departure, then slumped to the dirt, smoking and limp.

New confidence flooded Merek's blood, and he sprang up from the dirt, sword aloft, muscles tensed for the coming fight. He looked out over the sea of screaming skulls attached to wet, sleek bodies. All of them squatted in preparation to bound forward, empty eye sockets trained on him with pinpoint focus. He imagined those yellowed teeth sinking into the flesh of his arms, his legs, his neck, coming away stained with arterial blood. Merek imagined the life draining from him, the world going black as he fought to stay in it. His legs went wobbly. Even the magical weapon he held did not lend him the bravery to stand before this onslaught.

He was a farmer, not a soldier, but he was Rowan's father. He could not die now, not while his son might still be here, waiting for rescue. He turned on his heel and ran.

The forest bolted past him in a blur of black and gray and white. Trees and branches became tapestry hung in an infinitely and randomly turning hallway. The leaves below his feet crunched and crumbled in time with his footfalls and became a wall of sound in combination with the still air rushing past his ears.

The dogs were at his heels. Paws galloped and teeth clacked. They stopped screaming and emitted raspy, gargling breaths as they gave chase.

Merek slowed, the muscles in his legs burning, his lungs struggling. He knew in a moment the creatures would fall on him and rip the flesh from his bones. Doubtless he would become one of them himself, a gory fleshless skull doomed to run and scream in pure agony through the trees.

A black opening bloomed into sight beside the path. With the last of his strength, Merek dove toward it. He landed hard, skidding on his chest along the dirt floor of a darkened cave. He lay there in the cool dirt, fighting to breathe and waiting for those abominable beasts to fall upon him and begin their work.

They did not.

Several times, Merek lost consciousness, and in those moments, faces floated before him. First Rowan, playing with his horse in the yard and calling to him. Then Gwyddion, the old man, stood tall enough his shoulders brushed the hut's ceiling. Grinning, his eyes alight with green flame. Then his father, staring into these woods from the porch, full of fear. *Coward.*

It was dark when Merek lifted from his stupor. Dirt caked his face. His arm pulsed where the tree branch scratched him. His chest and legs were sore from the chase. He rolled onto his back and propped himself up so he could see his surroundings.

Through the arched cave mouth, Merek saw the trees. They were smooth and liquid again, highlighted blue in what Merek took for moonlight. A dim yellow glow emanated from his sword and illuminated his surroundings. Smooth, featureless rock formed the cave, the throat of which stretched off into blackness beyond the reach of the sword's glow.

Why did the hounds spare me? They were nipping at my heels. Why did they not follow? Merek reached over and grasped the sword, then raised it above his head like a torch. The light became brighter as if sensing Merek's intention. With great effort he pushed himself off the floor and to his feet, then turned in a circle, looking for anything he may have missed. All was smooth and unbroken.

Something caught his eye.

A small, brown lump on the ground, at the very edge of the light. It was easy to miss at the throat of the cave.

Merek moved toward it. He bent and brushed the dirt from

it, a sob fighting its way up from his chest. Rowan's wooden horse. Merek picked up the toy and held it to his chest. His body convulsed as tears spilled onto his cheeks. The horse was here because Rowan could not return for it, which must mean—

No.

Merek stood, gripping the sword in one hand and the toy in the other. He looked down the tunnel into infinite blackness. He would go into that gullet, into Hell itself, if that's where Rowan was. He would bring him back.

In that moment of conviction, a sound snaked from the darkness. A guttural growl that shook the walls and the floor. Merek planted his feet wide in the dirt. The glow from the sword brightened and the hilt was hot in Merek's hand.

He saw its eyes first. They glowed yellow in the dark. The thing stepped from the deep shadow. It was immense. The cave itself was three times as tall as Merek, and the creature stood hunched, its shoulders brushing the roof. Black hair covered its body, wet, caked, and matted. Its muscular arms, each as thick as a tree trunk, terminated in vicious talons large enough to encircle Merek's waist. The monster roared, and it sounded like pain and death and madness all together.

Merek raised his sword. This creature was here to keep him away from Rowan. It will fail.

Green ropes of saliva fell from its massive fangs and sizzled on the dirt at its feet.

"I am Merek, Father of Rowan, Guardian of the Black Wood, and you have taken my son."

The beast looked at Merek, its head lolled to one side.

"I have come to take him back." The sword danced in his palm, hungry for the monster's blood.

Merek leaped forward and swung. The creature stepped aside. Merek stumbled and fell past the beast. It batted him aside almost gently. Merek struck the cave wall. The wooden horse sprang from his grasp and clattered to the ground.

The beast plucked the toy and held it between two sharp

claws. Now was his chance. The thing stared at the toy, frozen with fascination.

Merek stood. He gripped the sword in both hands. Its power poured into him. The light from the hilt burned white. A scream of rage tore from his throat. He ran forward. There—its chest. An unguarded spot. Merek thrust with the blade. It slid deep, to the hilt. Wounded flesh sizzled and popped. The beast roared like a thunderstorm.

Merek yanked the weapon free. The stone on its hilt dimmed and the blade was suddenly heavy. Merek dropped it to the dirt.

The beast, screaming and flailing, appeared to shrink. It fell to its hands and knees, its hair receding, muscles atrophying, bones popping and crackling as they reconfigured into the form of a boy— no, of Rowan—clutching the toy horse to his tiny chest and breathing in wheezing gasps.

Merek crawled, shaking, across the dirt. *No.* the word repeated in his mind with rising intensity as he approached his son.

Rowan lay on his back, and stared at the ceiling. Blood poured from his chest and his eyes darted around, frightened, until they found the face of his father. "Daddy, you found him." Rowan raised the horse in one hand so Merek could see.

Merek gathered the boy up. Everything was a dim yellow blur. He stood and carried the bundle, his son, light as kindling for a fire, toward the cave's mouth. "Don't worry, you're okay. I've got you. You're okay. Let's go home. Oh, please, let's go home. Oh God, please let us go home and be okay."

Rowan was limp and unmoving. Merek listened to the boy's breathing as it wound down then stopped. He stumbled back against the smooth cave wall, and slid to the ground, still clutching the boy to his chest, and that is where he stayed.

SOME DAYS LATER—HE DID NOT COUNT BECAUSE HE DID NOT think—Merek woke to the sound of steel dragging across the cave floor. He had not moved since he'd slumped, had not let go of his son's body, which was now stiff and gray and cold in his arms. Merek looked up.

There Gwyddion stood, bathed in daylight from the cave mouth, holding the sword.

"This is too valuable an artifact to simply discard, Merek. I hope you won't be too angry with me if I keep it."

Merek's chapped lips stung as they parted. A dry croak escaped.

The old man stared. "This forest is full of secrets, you know. They are secrets that should rightfully be mine. I'm afraid I may have been a bit dishonest with you, friend." Gwyddion sat next to Merek and gave him a conspiratorial look. "You see, I told you the truth about your father, and the sword, and your line. You are the rightful guardian of this place, and young Rowan there would have followed along behind you and so on and so forth until time's end and all that interminable mess. But Merek, dear friend, your job was never to protect the village from the wood. Your *job* was to protect the wood from the village. Your job was to protect it from *me*. A job you have now failed at quite spectacularly, and much to my benefit."

Merek tried to move. In his mind, he grabbed the sword from the old man and readied himself to slice his throat where he sat, but his weak muscles could barely manage a twitch. He was close to death.

"No, no, don't get up. We're not quite through here." The old man stood and brushed the dirt from the rear end of his cloak. "You can see why I needed both of you gone. Couldn't chance you stumbling onto your destiny and all that. I thought it would be awfully poetic to have the boy rip his own father to pieces. But this is *much better*. Young boys are hard to master. They are willful and arrogant, they don't listen." Gwyddion made several quick, sharp motions with his hands in the air in front of himself.

The scratch on Merek's arm burned and he clenched his teeth against the scorch. His entire forearm had the black-green color of a fresh bruise. Something crawled, undulated beneath his skin. His bones popped, cracked, and moved. A scream tried in vain to escape his parched throat.

"You," said the old man, "will make a much better pet, I think."

THE CREATURE

There is a creature in the window. I stare at it, knowing only a single glass pane separates its teeth from my flesh. It stares at me knowing unfathomable things and coveting unknowable desires. Its breath fogs the thin barrier. I sweat in spite of the chill.

I should scream. I should run further into the house, barricade a door to a closet and wait until the danger has passed. But then how would I know if it ever did? No, I will stay here and meet the gaze of its bloodshot eyes.

Its face is human like mine, bearded like mine. It wears my glasses, my shirt but it isn't me. It is not of this world. It is violent, evil. It's done things I would never dream of. I have seen it hit and scream and hurt. I have seen it squeeze and flare and nearly kill only to pull back at that last vital moment. I have seen it fail to pull back, too. Its eyes turn red, go wide, and absorb the light around them until darkness devours everything but those eyes.

I have played with forces I do not understand. I have toyed with strange words in books that were not written for me. Or for any man. Through a long line of scholars and thieves and unlucky accidents they came to me, and like a fool I translated the text. I learned the language—first, how to read it, then how to speak it—and when I read aloud from the book's first page, the creature and I met. It stepped out of me, shaking, anxious for freedom, for purchase, traction, friction. It found those things and more.

It found blood.

It found meat.

It found pleasure.

For some reason, when it is not here, when we are separated by time and space, I believe I can stop it from coming again. But that's a lie. I tell myself that so I can sleep at night. But I can no more stop this creature from coming than I can stop myself from breathing. I think if I will myself to be more of something and less of something else I will never see the creature again. Foolish! The creature and I are tied like bone to tendon. To separate us is to kill us both.

But it has found me at home. Where I sleep.

It crouches like an animal against the black night, wet and cold and hungry. When its lips part there is a glimpse of teeth much sharper than mine. Its red tongue flicks out then back in, tasting the air. I think of what it will do when it enters. My wife is here, my daughters asleep in their rooms. They are peaceful.

I have told no one the creature exists. I have only run and hoped it wouldn't find me here, so if I don't protect them, they'll be defenseless. My babies will be awakened by their daddy only to be torn to shreds in their little beds and it will be as much my fault as the creature's. I will have murdered them through negligence and I will be damned to hell for it, which would be only right.

No. I reach for the glass on the table beside me and bring the bourbon to my lips. Its burn braces my bones, my muscles, my soul. It tells me I am doing the right thing. I set the tumbler back down and slide open the drawer below. Never unlocking my eyes from the creature's, I grope for the gun. My fist wraps around the handle and my finger finds the trigger. Some of Man's creations are so suited both to our bodies and our nature that to lift them, to hold them as they are meant to be held, is pure, exquisite pleasure. I feel that pleasure roll over me.

I wield this weapon in my family's defense, to reset the universe to its rightful configuration without this thing in it. I extend my hand in front of me and follow the line of the pistol with my eye. I aim for its eye. It grins.

This is a fantasy and I know it. This creature is not that fragile. I would be throwing a rock at a ghost. No, I invited it in, and it will take a sacrifice to rescind the invitation.

I let my hand, my arm, the gun go slack then drop to my lap for a moment before using every ounce of my will to raise it up again. This time I point it where it belongs. I press the cold barrel to my temple.

I never learned how to pray. What would I say? Do I ask for strength? Do I ask God to watch over my girls, my wife? Why would he do that when even I have played fast and loose with their lives? No. I have nothing to ask for. There is no help except that of my own will. If I am to protect them, I will have to sever the connection that keeps the creature here. There is only one way to do that.

The creature grins at me and through the gap in its lips I see what waits beneath the skin that looks like mine. Darkness writhes behind its shark teeth. I close my eyes and against the dark I see only my girls. My hand tightens again on the gun and I pause briefly as I hear the glass break.

This is for my babies.

THOSE WE LEFT BEHIND

His eyes are already open when his vision returns. There's a bright white flash. When it fades, he sees the glass front of his Hypersleep tube crisscrossed with reflections of the LED light bars that illuminate the round chamber beyond.

There's a deafening hiss, and the door slides open. He stretches, and his muscles burn. Pins and needles poke and prod and dig. He leans toward the opening and falls back.

A hulking shadow steps into view.

Doran, that asshole.

"Christ, Marcus, you better get up or you're gonna miss the bus." Doran laughs at his own joke, though nobody else listens. He saunters off, buck naked, toward the lockers.

The others stumble from their tubes into the gray metal room. Most, including Marcus, are civilian volunteers. None have ever been to space before, but all of them have an easier time than Marcus. The last person is across the room and into the lockers before he gets his feet under him.

Try again, he urges himself. It's easier now. The atrophied muscles in his thighs burn and twitch, but it's bearable. He stands and steps over the tube's lip. The cold metal is like an electric jolt to his soles. It's strange to walk.

Something skitters behind him.

He freezes. There's a tingle on his neck, and Marcus scratches it. Then he turns toward the door.

There's the deer, standing between Marcus and the door to the lockers. It's massive, and the highest points of its rack are just shy of touching the grated ceiling. It paws at the ground and snorts, steam exploding from its nostrils. Yellow light flashes in its eyes.

"You're—you're not here." Marcus has seen things like this before, but never this close, this real, and not for a long time.

It snorts again, and pounds its hoof against the floor, striking a deep metallic clang.

Marcus takes a step back.

The buck advances, teeth bared. They're sharp and strange—long needles that fold out of its mouth like the cilia on a Venus flytrap.

Marcus stumbles and falls. The deer is gone.

Doran stands in the locker room, towel wrapped around his waist, cackling with laughter. "Are you gonna make it, pussy?" He disappears back into the locker room, shaking his head.

Marcus rises and rubs his sore ass. Hypersleep side effects, he thinks.

MARCUS WAKES FROM A DEAD SLEEP. THERE'S NO SOUND, NO reason for him to be up in a cold sweat. The back of his neck tingles. Maybe that's what woke him—an itch. He scratches it.

He lies back on his mattress but can't get comfortable. Shit.

First night on a new world, and insomnia strikes. Tomorrow's shift will be a nightmare. After the Hypersleep wakeup, maintenance orientation, and everything else that happened this afternoon, he should be exhausted.

The room brims with snores. If they can sleep, why can't he?

Again, he swipes at his neck. What the hell is that?

His body urges him toward the window. He's careful not to wake the others.

The landscape isn't as red as he'd envisioned. Marcus imagined it brighter, the color of cherry candy or fresh blood. It's more of a ruddy brown.

Is that a person?

Volunteers aren't allowed off the ship. The only people permitted to go outside right now are the military contingent. There shouldn't be anyone there.

Marcus palms the frigid glass and leans in. His breath fogs then fades. Between the pulsing condensation, the night sky on mars is brilliant, shot through with so much starlight. And silhouetted against it is a boy who shouldn't be there.

It must be a rock formation playing tricks with the light. Nobody could survive Mars's elements without a suit.

The boy turns, walks to the side, and disappears behind a rocky outcrop.

Marcus thinks of the deer. No.

Wa—go—ho—ma—

Oh god, no. Sweat on Marcus's brow turns cold, and his body trembles.

The boy emerges closer to the ship. Exterior floodlights illuminate his shirt. It's maroon with white stripes.

The last time Marcus saw that shirt, it was soaked with blood. Jesse . . .

He stands on the red dirt, unmoving, hands at his sides, feet together like a toy soldier. Marcus can't see his face, but it doesn't matter. It's him.

This is in my head—something to do with Hypersleep. It has to be. Marcus stares until he can't anymore. When he wakes, Jesse is gone.

MARCUS DRIVES TOO FAST. THE NIGHT WHIPS PAST HIM LIKE A *reel of film. The trees on either side are a black-green blur. Wind from the open window rumbles in Marcus's ear and sucks his cigarette smoke out into the night; he imagines it leaving a trail like an old-fashioned locomotive.*

It's only a couple miles now, and he gets to drop Jesse off, send his weepy ass into the house where he belongs so he can go back out and keep being a big man. Jesse can tell Mama how mean he's been. Marcus will catch it when he gets home, but for tonight Mama can't get him because he's got a car and a place to go, booze to drink, a girl to fuck—maybe. It's not fair he got saddled with Jesse in the first place.

Marcus looks at his brother. The lights from the dashboard trace him, reflect off the sheen of tears on his cheeks like gossamer cloth.

Jesse lets out a sob. It's the first noise he's made since they got in the car back at the party.

Marcus gets angry. It's irrational, a wild rage that corners his higher brain functions and takes control. Alcohol doesn't help. It runs underneath all his thoughts, numbing his conscience. His muscles roil and flex like irritated snakes. "Say something, you little shit," Marcus says through gritted teeth.

Jesse raises his hand to his face and rubs his eyes.

"You're always crying about something." He flicks the cigarette butt out the window and watches the wind turn the cherry into a trail of sparks that dip and swirl in the air like passing comets. "Answer me!" Marcus reaches over and punches his brother's shoulder.

Jesse cries out, then sobs again, louder. "Fucking bully," he says, then sniffs the drainage back into his nose. It's a child's insult, but he is a child —just thirteen. He should be at home, already asleep, but he insisted. He told Mama he wanted to go out with his big brother.

If Marcus had told her where he was going, why Jesse shouldn't come, Mama would have shut the whole thing down. Jesse wanted to go out and party with the big kids, but instead, he freaked out, and now Marcus has to carry him home. He'll be lucky if there's still any pussy waiting for him at that party when he gets back.

Marcus punches again, harder this time. Jesse raises a hand to defend himself, but Marcus keeps attacking. Jesse's face bunches up in pain and fear, and then he screams.

Marcus turns his attention back to the road in time to see the deer, its eyes flashing yellow in the headlights, its front hooves stamping like it's preparing for battle.

"Marcus!" Jesse screams.

Marcus pulls the wheel right, and the tires leave the road.

MARCUS SETS HIS TRAY DOWN ALONE AT THE END OF A LONG metal table. The mess hall is quiet. It's like the whole ship is holding its breath. There are armed military guards, one in each corner of the room, who weren't there at the beginning of the week.

Two hundred and twenty-seven people came to Mars from Earth to start a colony, new lives. A week later, there are two hundred and nineteen.

Marcus stirs the gray protein-mush on his plastic lunch tray. The only sounds are chewing and cutlery clattering. Nobody speaks. The silence is deliberate, strained. Then it breaks.

"God dammit!"

It's Doran.

He's sitting three tables away, surrounded by silent people who stare at him, wide-eyed. He punches the table, and lunch trays jump. One falls to the ground; its owner scrambles to clean up the mess. The guards, who before looked around lazily, snap to attention and focus on Doran.

"Why won't anybody talk to me?" He stands, pushing his stool backward with a metallic screech. "It's like living in a fucking morgue! Don't any of you see it? It's fucking with us.

We've got to figure out what's going on! Marissa, Taylor—what was that other guy's name? Paul? They're not here. Something's got them! All of us are gonna die if we don't do something. I know you know what I'm talking about. I know you've seen it."

The guards rush toward him. Two of them rest their hands on their sidearms.

Doran looks down. "It—it looks like my mom," his tone is different. There's no bravado, no anger. Something has shaken him.

The guards surround him, and there is a bout of frantic whispering. One puts a hand on Doran's chest.

His face blooms red. Then he slaps his tray off the table, sending gray mush splattering. "You know what? Fuck you guys." Doran pushes a guard aside and storms across the room to the door.

When he's gone, a few voices murmur to each other, then subside, returning the room to relative silence.

Marcus stares after him. This is the first real confirmation that it's not just him, that others are seeing things. Doran's right. Something *is* messing with them, and it's the reason eight people are missing. How did he not put it together?

Marcus gets up quietly, leaving his tray on the table, and makes for the door. Nobody looks up as he passes.

The door out of the mess leads to a long corridor that extends in both directions. Marcus looks left, then right. No sign of Doran. He holds his breath, listens. There. It's faint, but—is that crying? Marcus follows the sound down the hallway to the bathrooms. He presses a button, and the door slides open.

"Doran?"

The crying halts.

"Doran, I know you're in here."

"Get out." His voice comes from the stalls.

Marcus steps toward them. "C'mon, man, it's all right. I just want to talk."

Doran snorts. He's in the third stall from the left.

Marcus grabs the handle and rattles it, hoping Doran left it unlocked. "Doran, I've seen it too. You're right. We need to figure out what's happening."

With a sharp bang, the stall door flies open. Doran is out; he grabs Marcus's jumpsuit and wads a chunk of it in his fist. Doran shoves Marcus backward, thumping him into the wall. His eyes are wild, his shoulders rising and falling with each ragged breath.

"What the hell do you want from me?"

This was not the reaction Marcus expected, but he's not sure *what* he expected. Was Doran, the same guy who's been a complete asshole to him since training, supposed to have a change of heart now?

"Answer me! Did you want to catch me crying? You got your cam on?" Doran's face turns red again, his shaking fist drawn back like he's going to punch Marcus in the face.

"No! No."

"Then what?"

"I saw my little brother."

Doran's muscles relax. His shoulders drop. He loosens his grip on Marcus's jumpsuit.

Marcus pulls away from him and tries to smooth the fabric.

"I'm—I'm sorry," Doran says.

"What the hell, man?"

"I dunno. I'm sorry I grabbed you. It's just—I guess I'm tired. I haven't been sleeping."

There are bags under Doran's bloodshot eyes. The creases next to his mouth and nose seem deeper, darker.

"You saw your mom?" Marcus asks.

"Yeah. Weirdest fucking thing. She stands outside in her housedress. No suit or anything. She's far away, but she's staring at me."

Marcus nods.

"Same for my brother. Did your mom—is she—"

"Dead? Yeah. She died right before I came up here. How about your brother?"

"Yeah. Car wreck when we were kids. I'd just got my license."

Doran nods. "So I guess it's safe to assume neither of them is up here on Mars, right?"

"I think so," Marcus says.

"Yeah, me too. But something is."

"Yeah."

"You think the other people see stuff too?"

"I think that's why nobody's talking."

"So what the hell are we gonna do?"

Marcus shakes his head. He was hoping Doran had a plan.

"I'll tell you what I'm gonna do," Doran says. "I'm gonna go for a little stroll. Outside. And if that thing comes anywhere near me, I'm gonna snap its neck. You coming?"

Marcus's body is on fire. His world is sideways. He opens his eyes through a crust of blood.

He's in the car. Jesse's not.

Marcus opens his mouth to call out to his brother, but his throat is dry, closed. He only manages a frog-like croak.

The car is at the bottom of a ditch, roof pressed against the tree that stopped it cold. Marcus dangles from the seatbelt. He gropes around with his sticky fingers and finds the buckle. His thumb mashes the button, and he tumbles, striking the center console and turning, so his head hits the passenger door. He lays for a moment in a pile of shattered glass. The shards grind into his shoulder through his t-shirt.

He turns so his legs point down. The ruined sedan groans around him. The smell of gasoline, hot metal, and burnt plastic hangs thick in the air. He puts his feet underneath him and stands.

His left leg is a column of pure fire, and a scream tears itself from his throat. He pushes on the windshield. It's solid. He needs to climb up through the driver's side window. It's the only way out, the only way to Jesse.

Marcus raises his good leg and steps on the console. His left shoulder goes numb. Glass digs into his palms as he pulls himself up.

The night breeze blows cool against his skin, made even colder by blood-soaked clothes that cling to him. He jumps down from the car and lands on his left foot. A bomb detonates in his hip, and he cries out again, then falls to the ground. "Jesse!"

There's no response, just the car's engine ticking as it cools. Then the grass rustles and a soft moan comes from the hill above. Marcus crawls toward it.

By the time he reaches his brother, Marcus is biting his bottom lip to keep from passing out. The pain contracts his vision, so he's crawling through a black tunnel. The sight of Jesse lying on his back, half on, half off the road, snaps him out of it.

There is too much blood. Jesse convulses. A puff of red smoke escapes his lips and disperses into the cold air.

Marcus crawls on top of him. "Oh, Jesus. Oh, fuck."

One of Jesse's eyes is closed. The other rolls wildly in his skull. His face is shiny with blood that pumps out in rivulets from the wound on his head. It's caved in, his brain is exposed. Jesse mumbles. His breathing is shallow and quick. "Ma—ma—ho—wa—go—"

Marcus puts a hand on Jesse's chest. "Jesse, I'm here. It's Marcus. Try not to talk. Can you hear me?" Tears blur Marcus's vision, he blinks them away.

"Ho—was—go—ma—"

"It's okay, little man. It's gonna be okay. I'm right here."

"Ho—wa—"

"What are you saying?"

Jesse's rolling eye stops and focuses on Marcus's face. "I wanna—go home. Mama, I—wanna go—home." Jesse loses his focus again, tracking something nobody but him can see.

"It's okay. I'm gonna get you home." Marcus reaches for his phone and then he checks for Jesse's. They're still in the car. Marcus hadn't even thought to grab it before he climbed out. He'll have to go back into the

wreck, find a phone and call for help. He'll never make it and it wouldn't matter. Blood is soaking the road under Jesse's head, pooling, running off into the grass. His shirt is drenched in it.

Marcus won't let his brother live his life as a vegetable. He won't let him suffer. "It's okay, Jesse. You're almost home. Just a little further." Marcus pinches Jesse's nose between his thumb and forefinger and covers his mouth with his palm. "Almost there."

Jesse trembles underneath him, then bucks. His open eye is wide, aimed straight at Marcus. Hot tears run down Marcus's face mixing with the thick blood. Fat, red droplets fall onto Jesse's cheeks.

"Almost home."

"Mm—mm—mm—"

"Not long now."

Jesse's body gives a final shudder, and then he's still. His eye rolls to the side and settles, staring downhill toward the car.

Marcus's chest heaves. He gulps air like he's been underwater. Jesse is dead. It was mercy. Please, God, let it have been mercy. Marcus rolls off his brother. His vision tunnels again, and the world grows smaller. Blackness washes over him; pure bliss. Maybe he'll die, too.

"You're home," Marcus whispers to the night sky.

IN THE LOCKER ROOM NEXT TO THE AIRLOCK, DORAN HAS LAID out two vac suits, one large and the other smaller, on the metal bench. Next to each is a crowbar.

Marcus shakes his head. "How'd you do this?"

"There's a military guy in my bunk room. I . . . *borrowed* his access card."

"And we're just going to go out there and beat that thing to death?"

"That's the plan."

"Your mom. You're gonna beat your mom to death with a crowbar?"

"It's not my mom."

"I know, but it—"

"It's not my fucking mom, jerkoff. You got me? And that's not your brother either. I don't know what happened that's got you all tied up, and I'll tell you, I don't really give a shit. You need to focus. We both know damn well my mom, your brother —they're dead. They're rotting in the ground in some bullshit cemetery on a whole other planet. They damn sure aren't standing around on the surface of Mars watching through the windows. Whatever they are, they're using the people we left behind—violating them, dragging them out of the ground, messing with our heads."

Doran's right. Marcus knows it. "I killed him, you know." It's quiet while Marcus gathers his thoughts. How much does he want to share with Doran? Does it matter? Marcus shakes his head. "No, you're right. I'm coming. You know, the first time I saw it, it wasn't even my brother. It was a deer. I was thinking about the wreck, so it became the deer—the one I swerved to avoid."

Doran laughs. It's different, less mocking, born of relief, a kind of affirmation. Marcus laughs, too. If there's any doubt left in either of them, it melts away in that moment.

They suit up in silence. Marcus fastens the clear helmet onto his vac suit and grips the crowbar.

"You ready?" Doran asks.

"Yeah. Let's do it."

"We've got about two minutes until shift change is over. If we get caught, we'll be in the brig for a month."

MARS'S SURFACE IS A MASSIVE, JAGGED EXPANSE BENEATH A star-strewn blackness deeper than any sky Marcus has ever known. The view from the windows didn't prepare him for how small he would feel.

Marcus looks back at the ship. It was designed to be their

home for months after landing. It folded out of itself, anchored into the rock, leveled on mechanical legs like a monstrous pop-up camper. From out here, it's as big as a town.

He's sure they are being watched, and not by anything human. The itch on his neck resurfaced the moment they stepped out of the airlock. "It's close," Marcus says.

"You feel it too?"

"Same thing every time." Marcus raises his hand to his neck. "I think that's how it knows what to show us."

"Wherever this thing goes to ground, it's got to be near the ship," Doran says. His voice crackles, staticky, over the helmet coms.

Doran points ahead, and they walk in silence, sticking close to the ship, its massive shadowy underside to their left. In some places, the space is more than tall enough for them to stand upright, and in others, it's little more than a crawlspace. To their right is a vast red desert.

Marcus grits his teeth. Hot needles jab his neck. Underneath the ship, it's full dark, so he turns on his helmet light.

There is Jesse, crawling on his stomach, staring at him with black eyes. Marcus jumps back, pinwheeling his arms to avoid falling. Doran grabs his shoulder.

Jesse is gone.

"You all right?"

"It's—it's under there."

"Shit, I was afraid of that." Doran turns his light on. "Where was it?"

Marcus points.

"Tight fit. We're gonna have to crawl. Be careful. Don't tear your suit." Doran ducks and army crawls, disappearing under the ship.

Marcus hesitates. He's never liked confined spaces.

Doran's voice comes through his helmet, "If I have to come back out there and get you, I'm gonna cave your fucking helmet in."

Marcus squats. It's not that tight, maybe three feet from the rocky ground to the ship's smooth underside. His chest tightens. For a moment he's in the car again, contorted steel crowding in around him. He takes a deep breath. "Okay, I'm coming in."

He creeps into the dark. The suit makes it feel like he's crawling through thick sludge. It's a Herculean effort to push himself forward. His powerful helmet lamp seems anemic down here, struggling to illuminate even a narrow strip in front of him. How far in did Doran go? He's been crawling for a few seconds, or has it been a minute? There's nothing but rocks and dirt, the same in every direction. No landmark breaks the uniformity. It's maddening. He can't see Doran, doesn't know which direction he went.

There's a scuttling sound, a series of rhythmic ticks, which doesn't make sense because the vac suit should isolate him from outside sound. Or was that in his head?

Something on the suit snags against a rock, arresting his forward motion.

Fuck.

His leg is stuck. He pulls but it doesn't come free.

Marcus jerks upward and his helmet strikes the ship's underside with a hollow *thonk*. Marcus imagines being found down here in a year or two, a mummy in a vac suit tied to a rock, sandwiched between the ship and the ground. His heart hammers in his chest and his breathing becomes erratic.

"You all right back there?" Doran asks.

"Yeah, fine."

"Sounds like you're running a marathon." Doran's laugh is mocking.

Marcus's neck sears as if someone stabbed him. He grits his teeth, holds back a scream. What the hell? "Jesse?"

"Who?" Doran's tone is cynical.

"No—nobody."

Jesse's face floats in front of Marcus in the dark, and it's like he never left the roadside. Marcus stares at his brother's pulsing brain through the fist-sized hole in his skull. He smells the gasoline, hears the ticking engine.

"Holy shit." Doran pulls him from the visage. "Man, no wonder this thing's pissed. We parked right on top of its house. You need to get over here."

Marcus shakes his head, trying to clear the residual images. Stop. He takes a deep breath and reaches down to his leg. There. A circular piece of plastic protrudes from the suit's leg and it's stuck on a sharp rock. He pushes it aside, and he can move again. He quickens his pace and then sees Doran who's lying on his side next to a mound of stones. Marcus squints as Doran's helmet lamp cuts across his face, blinding him. When his vision returns, Doran is motioning to him to come closer.

"Dude, you're gonna hate this."

Marcus nears and sees it's not a mound. It's a hole about two feet wide dug downward at an angle. It's deep enough that the light from Marcus's helmet lamp doesn't make it to the bottom.

"We're not—"

"Oh, we are."

"No. Doran, I—"

"Then go back inside or wait here alone. I'm gonna go bag me a critter. Follow me if you want." Doran scrambles into the hole, crowbar gripped like a medieval mace, and he's gone.

Fuck. Marcus follows him in a downward slide.

The dirt walls of the tunnel are close. There isn't enough room to turn around. The ceiling scrapes his helmet. His heart flutters and jumps in his chest. He's breathing so fast he's light-headed. We're so fucked. That thing better be down here.

And it is. He knows it is. He can feel it. In the back of his mind, it repeats Jesse's last sputtering syllables.

Marcus grasps for another handful of dirt and touches nothing but open space. He gropes and finds the tunnel's sides, then yanks himself free, dropping into a chamber. He can stand. The sensation eases him somewhat.

"Doran?"

No answer. Maybe their location is interfering with the helmet coms? He scans the area and appears to be in a stone chamber. The walls are smooth and mostly free of dirt. The room is cube-shaped.

"No way."

The place looks carved out by humans. Marcus reminds himself where he is. Markings are on the wall to his left, but he can't understand them. They're too consistent to be random scratches. Piles of what look like sticks sit in the corners. Bones. Those are bones. There's too many of them to just be the eight people missing from the ship—and they're too old.

Ma—wa—go—ho—

Jesse's chanted syllables are more urgent, louder, drowning his thoughts. The back of his neck throbs in time with his pulse.

Doran.

An opening on the far side leads to a narrow corridor. Doran must have gone through there. It's the only way out. Numerous open rooms flank the hallway, filled with more heaps of discarded bones. In one, there's a body in a vac suit lying discarded, fresh, limbs flung wide in contorted abandon. The face is frozen, mouth dropped open in an eternal scream. The eyes are gone, scooped from its skull.

"Christ—it's Paul."

Static explodes over his helmet speaker.

"Marcus! Marcus, you there? Did you make it down? I've got it cornered!"

"Doran, where are you? I—I found a body."

"Don't worry about that. Get over here, I need you. Follow the hallway. I'm in the big room at the end. I think we can take this thing."

Marcus shuffles as fast as he can, but it's like wading through waist-deep mud. The corridor twists and turns, then ends, exploding into a massive hall. Doran stands in the middle of the room, chest heaving, crowbar raised over his head. Jesse crouches below him, arm raised to protect his face.

It's not Jesse. Right?

Ma—go—wa—ho—

"You made it," Doran says. "Get over here and help me."

Wa—ho—mm—mm—

Jesse's lips are moving, but the sound is inside Marcus's head. He's back in the car, going too fast. The trees on all sides of him are a blur. There's a curve in the road. He doesn't let off the gas. There's the deer. Yellow headlights in its eyes.

"Marcus!" Jesse screams.

Marcus's crowbar comes down.

"What the fu—" Doran says, eyes wide.

The tool makes contact with Doran's helmet, and Marcus's arm vibrates. The glass spiderwebs.

Doran screams. "No, don't!"

"Don't touch my brother, you son of a bitch!" Marcus brings the crowbar down again, and the glass shatters.

Doran screams and the crowbar clangs to the floor. He gropes forward, trying to grab onto the front of Marcus's vac suit, but Marcus steps back, out of reach. A retching, gagging sound comes over Marcus's helmet com.

Marcus swings the crowbar again. This time it makes contact with flesh. Doran's cheekbone crumples beneath the blow, and he falls.

"Don't touch him!" Marcus swings again and again.

Bright red arcs of gore come up with the crowbar as he raises it for another strike. When he's done, Doran's face is replaced by a mash of pink and red foam in the bottom of the helmet. Marcus drops his crowbar.

A single small beep sounds from his helmet com.

Low oxygen.

Too much heavy breathing. He won't make it out, doesn't want to. Marcus turns to Jesse. He's perfect except for those black eyes.

"I saved you. This time I saved you."

Jesse tilts his head.

Marcus walks toward him. All these years, he's been running, from Jesse, from that night. He hasn't stopped since the moment he woke up in the hospital with the memory of what he did, what he still believes he had to do.

Marcus drops to his knees. "I love you, Jesse." He wraps his arms around the boy, pulls him close. Jesse feels solid, real. He even smells right, like sunshine and yard dirt. Marcus knows it's all in his head. The spot on his neck burns. He doesn't care.

There's a sound like tearing fabric, and a bulky insectile arm emerges from behind Jesse's back. Its tip is as big and sharp as a Bowie knife. Then another materializes, then another. Marcus loses count through the blur of tears. The extraterrestrial limbs encircle him and hug him tight. Jesse's mouth opens, exposing a battery of needle-like fangs that flare outward. Marcus closes his eyes and concentrates on the feeling of his brother in his arms, warm and alive. Jesse's heart beats against him.

The back of his suit splits, and the air is sucked from his body. He tries to scream, but the saliva on his tongue boils and sizzles down to his lungs and into his chest. A talon pierces his spine, digs until there's a crunch. Immense pain flares, his body jerks, senses float away, and in the void, there's a voice.

We're home, Marcus. We're home.

STORY NOTES

If you haven't read the stories in this book already, I'd suggest you do so before reading my notes. Spoilers abound.

BEDTIME STORY

ORIGINALLY PUBLISHED IN WRITTEN TALES, JUNE 2020

This story started with the title. I read in Ray Bradbury's wonderful craft memoir, *Zen In The Art Of Writing*, that one of his ideation exercises consisted of writing down as many titles as possible and then using them as writing prompts.

I, at the time, was going through a bit of a slump, and so I decided to go online and find a story title generator. "Bedtime Story" came up, and immediately, Peter Falk from *The Princess Bride* jumped to mind. Then I thought, "what if the grandpa was dead the whole time?"

THE PAPER ON WHICH WE ALL ARE DRAWN

The drawing I reference in this book is real. It's a Stephen Gammell drawing from the book *Scary Stories to Tell In The Dark*, specifically for the story "The Walk" by Alvin Schwartz. The story is innocuous, even silly, but I remember sitting in my room at night, terrified to look out the window next to my bed, afraid that I would see the smudgy black figure next to our tree in the back yard. I still get a little shock in my chest whenever I peel open my blinds and look out into the night. Stephen Gammell is a genius. I suppose this story is my homage to the effect he had on me that has lasted decades.

TEA PARTY

There is nothing more frightening to me than my nine-year-old daughter. She is a ball of will and fury that challenges me at every step, and all I want in life is to love her and keep her safe. So much of Maddie in this story is informed by her. Of course, my daughter would never hurt me. She loves me a lot. We love each other. But what if I did something unforgivable in her eyes? Would she turn cold? Vindictive? I hope I never find out.

Honestly, this story originated as something of a dad joke. The first scene I wrote was the last one, from Maddie's point of view. I wanted to write a story around the joke about "finger sandwiches." Womp womp.

Despite that, I feel like this evolved into one of my more frightening stories, which is why I put it close to the front in this collection. It still gives me chills.

THE LAST DAYS OF THE OLD MAN

ORIGINALLY PUBLISHED IN LITERALLY LITERARY, JANUARY 2020

This is not a horror story. It's more weird magical adventure, if that's a thing. It was, however, intended to be part of a larger series of loosely connected stories, two of which are included in this book, and skew more recognizably toward the horror genre. One is "A Little Break," and the other is "The Black Wood." See if you can spot the connection. I included "The Last Days..." here partially for context, and also to break up the mood. I hope you don't mind. It's the only story I was nervous to include.

Subsequently, this is the only story I ever wrote on Medium that was curated under the fiction category, meaning that one of their curators read it and deemed it worthy to be actively promoted to their reader base. It's sort of like Medium's equivalent to traditional publishing. I hope that means people liked it.

ROOTS RUN DEEP

This story was written for an eco-horror anthology call, although I ended up withdrawing it to include it in this book. The original concept was probably closer to what they meant by "eco-horror" —where the source of the horror is actually the plants—but my stories tend to be more relationship oriented, and I'm a pantser, so here we are.

At its root (pun!) this is a story about how love can make us do crazy things. Would you kill to have it? Would you die?

THE GOAT MAN

I was chatting with a friend about her submission to an urban legend anthology, and how her story focused on a legend from her home town, and that got me thinking about the Goat Man. He's a character that I believe is pretty ubiquitous in Texas, especially in small towns where the teenagers have nothing better to do than drive to some remote spot in the middle of the country and drink.

The legend of the Goat Man goes like this: you park your car on the bridge, turn off your lights and your engine, and honk three times. Then, the Goat Man will come out from under the bridge and carry you off.

Our bridge was just a little concrete thing that didn't even have guardrails running over a shallow creek, and it was out in the middle of an expansive cow pasture on a county road. The night out there is so dark, and the sky is so big. Anyway, I drove out there once and tried it. Unfortunately, there was no Goat Man. Real life is often disappointing that way, which is why I do this.

IN THE TREES

ORIGINALLY PUBLISHED IN CROW & CROSS KEYS, JANUARY 2021

This is maybe my most personal story. It is certainly one of my favorites. The house, land, woods, and road are all based on where I grew up. The woods were smaller, and only bordered one side of the property, but all woods are big when you're little.

It was deliberately written in the style of a Grimm's fairy tale, right down to the repeated use of the word "and" instead of comma-delimitated lists—something I took great pains to improve in the editing process.

The final lines of this story are among my favorite things I have ever written. Being a kid is hard, almost always.

ELEVATOR

ORIGINALLY PUBLISHED IN FROST ZONE ZINE, ISSUE 1, SEPTEMBER 2020

I wrote this story in about an hour. I suppose what was in the back of my mind at the time was the scene in the movie The Eye with the man on the elevator. Seriously, if you haven't seen that, the whole movie is great, but that one scene has stuck with me for years. I just added a kid, which, to me, makes everything scarier.

Of all my stories, this one is the most like a joke, in that there is a setup and a punchline. A lot of flash fiction works that way, but this was the first time I pulled it off. Funny enough, I thought it would get a laugh, but that hasn't been the reaction that folks have communicated back to me.

A LITTLE BREAK

ORIGINALLY PUBLISHED IN MIDNIGHT MOSAIC FICTION, FEBRUARY 2020

I am a terrible introvert. That means that I "recharge my batteries" by being alone. It's an interesting predicament for a man with a wife and two daughters. Lucky for me, my wife is very kind. She will, once or twice a year, take the kids and go visit her parents, leaving me behind to lay around and watch TV, write, and play video games for the weekend. It is something I am immensely grateful for, and also feel terribly guilty about. I wanted to write a story about someone with the same proclivities as myself, but with something terrible happening by the end of the story.

See if you can spot the connection with "The Last Days Of The Old Man." When I wrote these two stories, I had a connected short story universe in mind. There was going to be a third story involving Clay from "The Last Days..." and his investigation into some relevant, gruesome murders. Maybe there still will be.

THE OPEN MOUTH

ORIGINALLY PUBLISHED IN LITERALLY LITERARY, NOVEMBER 2019

Have you ever stood in a dark room holding a screaming baby? If you're a parent, probably. If you're not, let me tell you, that will screw with your head something rotten. I used to stare at the black hole of my daughter's wailing mouth and imagine it growing in the dim blue nightlight glow. I would always stop myself before she swallowed me.

THE CREATURE

ORIGINALLY PUBLISHED IN MIDNIGHT MOSAIC FICTION, DECEMBER 2019

It wasn't until after I'd written this story that someone pointed out to me it could be allegorical. That happens sometimes. You think you're writing a straightforward story about a guy looking at a monster doppelgänger outside his window, and what you're *really* writing is a Jeckyl and Hyde story about a guy confronting the darkest corners of himself and deciding to kill himself over it. Go figure.

Writing (or art of any kind, really) is sort of like a Rorschach test. What the artist puts on the page, and what the reader sees, are often reflections of things they see in themselves. For me, that works especially well when I'm not paying attention.

YOU WILL BE THE ONE TO FIND THIS

ORIGINALLY PUBLISHED IN LITERALLY LITERARY, AUGUST 2019

This was one of the first things I wrote when I got serious about wanting to pursue writing. I still love it deeply. It was written for a Medium publication called *The Weekly Knob* that would give single-word prompts. This week's prompt was "jar." I didn't make the deadline for that week, so I didn't submit it to them, but I liked the story enough that I sent it to another outlet.

So many of the *things* in this book are real. The house this story takes place in is my grandmother's house. Part of this is remembering my mom and her sisters going through all of my grandfather's personal effects after he died. The other part is, years before all that, my cousins and I really did knock over a big conch shell in that living room once. My grandma made us sit on the floor without talking for a whole hour as punishment. Nobody died as a result.

AND THE REVEL WENT WHIRLINGLY ON

ORIGINALLY PUBLISHED IN WRITTEN TALES MAGAZINE, VOLUME 1, AUGUST, 2020

I wrote this story while I was at work. Don't tell my boss. I wrote it specifically for the prompt "renewal" which was the theme of the first issue of Written Tales Magazine. The first line of the story is the first thing that jumped into my mind when I gave the term any thought.

Fun fact: I wrote this maybe a month before the COVID-19 pandemic became news. Didn't even know it was coming. I often wonder if there were things that were dropped into my subconscious by news I watched or articles I read, kind of like the way magicians will guess what you're going to say or pick by having placed subliminals in the environment. Or maybe I'm some kind of prophet. Who knows?

THE BLACK WOOD

ORIGINALLY PUBLISHED IN LITERALLY LITERARY, AUGUST 2020

I used to write 50-word microfiction for a Medium publication called *The Friday Fix*. The idea was that they would give you a prompt each week, and you had to write fifty words exactly—no more, no less. I usually made it as creepy as I could, but this week I chose a straightforward fantasy direction. The microfiction story I wrote was called "So Am I Sworn" and it went:

I stand before the beast that took them from me, and though it is large and has claws so sharp they could scrape my soul from my bones, I raise my sword. The monster bares its teeth. I swear that it will taste its own blood before it tastes mine.

I got a lot of comments on it, several of them encouraging me to turn it into a longer story. "The Black Wood" was the eventual result and it came from the thought, "what if the missing son was the monster?" So many of my stories are about parental failure, but I think this one examines the theme more than most. Merek is so focused on the idea of saving his son from the monster that he fails to see the situation for what it really is, and his child pays the price, as they so often do.

This was one of the few times when I knew the theme ahead of time and made choices very specifically based on it.

DRAIN

ORIGINALLY PUBLISHED IN MIDNIGHT MOSAIC FICTION, JANUARY 2020

Stephen King very famously said, "I recognize terror as the finest emotion and so I will try to terrorize the reader. But if I find that I cannot terrify, I will try to horrify, and if I find that I cannot horrify, I'll go for the gross-out. I'm not proud." This story was my own very conscious decision to go for the gross-out.

Showers have always freaked me out. The spider story is

something real that actually happened to me, and my parents still make fun of me for it. There was also a story I read a long time ago about a water spirit that sucks a kid down a shower drain. I don't remember what it was called or where I read it (if you know the one, please DM me on Twitter or email me through my website, because I'd love to find it), but boy did it ever stick. Mix that all up into a soup and you get this icky little number.

THOSE WE LEFT BEHIND

This story changed drastically between concept and execution. My original idea was to have the main character as someone whose job it was to watch the camera feed from a Mars rover. This guy would then see his dead little brother standing on the surface of Mars. I had a ton of trouble with the concept, mostly around creating danger for the protagonist. I probably stopped and restarted writing this story a dozen times. Things really took off, however, when I just put the protagonist on Mars, especially when I put the deer in the hypersleep room.

The other trouble I had was with how to get the characters into the monster's lair without them going on a long boring walk across the featureless Martian landscape. It was my wife who eventually suggested that ship should be parked on top of the hole.

CONTENT WARNINGS

These content warnings are presented as a courtesy for those who would like to use them for any reason at all. Please note, they may contain mild spoilers.

- **Bedtime Story** - Suicide, spouse death, child murder, war
- **The Paper On Which We All Are Drawn** - Domestic stress
- **Tea Party** - Parenting fears, suicide, cannibalism, mutilation
- **The Last Days Of The Old Man** - Death, fire
- **Roots Run Deep** - tight spaces, murder, plant-based horror (botanophobia)
- **The Goat Man** - domestic abuse, suicide, enclosed spaces
- **In The Trees** - Domestic abuse, child abuse, death
- **Elevator** - Parenting fears, stalking, home invasion
- **A Little Break** - Death, blood, implied domestic violence, slugs
- **The Open Mouth** - Blood, death, child-related violence

- **The Creature** - Suicide, domestic violence, mental illness
- **You Will Be The One To Find This** - Parent death, cancer, self-harm
- **And The Revel Went Whirlingly On** - Classism, death, blood, disease, isolation
- **The Black Wood** - Kidnapping/abduction, child death
- **Drain** - Domestic abuse, murder, blood, gore, childbirth, death
- **Those We Left Behind** - Vehicle wreck, murder, sibling death, tight spaces, suffocation

ACKNOWLEDGMENTS

When I first started writing, I was sure it would be a solitary activity. I had an image of myself in a tweed jacket with patches on the elbows in a room stacked with books and loose papers, gazing at the world through my window but basking in isolation.

Turns out that whole idea is bullshit.

It takes the help of a ton of people to put together a book, even when most of it is already written. I would not have been able to do this, whatever it's worth, without the help of my friends.

Cassandra Yorke, author of the fantastic novel *Mary, Everything*, was the first stranger (at the time—happily, we are no longer strangers) who ever reached out and told me that a story of mine meant something to her. It was "In The Trees." I'm grateful she saw the same heart in that story that beats in much of her own work. Thanks, Cassie, for caring, for beta reading several of the stories in this book, and for putting so much thought and effort into the beautiful text treatment for the cover.

Elford Alley, author of several short story collections and novels including *Find Us*, *In Search Of The Nobility*, *TX Wildman*, and most recently *We Will Find A Place For You*, has been one of my most ardent supporters for a long time—ever since he volunteered to beta read my story "Those We Left Behind." He's read several of my stories since then, beta read this book, and I don't think he has ever missed an opportunity to talk me up or to offer sage advice. Thanks, Elford, for your support, your guidance, your encouraging if slightly overzealous use of exclamation marks, and for writing the foreword for this book. You've done a lot to make me believe I can actually do this whole writing thing. I hope one day I'll be able to repay you for all that.

Alexis DuBon, author of numerous short stories, including credits in Horror Oasis, The Dish, and *Field Notes From A Nightmare* from Dread Stone Press, said it best when she told me "I'm your pep rally." Aside from the fact that she's way more than that (if you want to know what kind of complete badass she is, go read her story in *Field Notes*), she was right. But she usually is. She pushed me to tighten my writing, to reach out to others in the industry to get blurbs and reviews ("they're just people"), and to do a better job at putting this book together than I ever intended to do at the start. She is a ruthless critique partner and a steadfast friend. Thank you for listening to me go on, for celebrating my victories with me, and for pushing me as hard as you could. I'll do the same for you whenever you need it.

Thanks also to **Rena Mason**, for your mentorship through the HWA, and for not pulling your punches. Rena beat several of the stories in this book into shape, and if it weren't for her, I'd still be writing in passive voice and repeating myself all over the place. I'd also still be trying to do this by myself. Thanks, Rena, for opening my world up.

Christopher Castillo Díaz's cover art is phenomenal. He perfectly captured what I was hoping to do right away and was a breeze to work with. You can find him just about everywhere (I found him on Fiverr, but he's also on Facebook and Instagram) under the alias Artem Asteroth (artem_astaroth), and if you need artwork for your project, I would suggest you seek him out.

Thank you **Eric Raglin**, **Gordon B. White**, **Red Lagoe**, **Joshua Marsella**, **Patrick Barb**, and **Alex Ebenstein** for your wonderful blurbs, reviews, and kind words of encouragement. If I can ever do anything to help any of you with your future projects, please, please let me know.

Thanks to **Jim Clark** for helping me navigate Goodreads so I could collect some early reviews.

Thank you to **Raul Reads and Steve Talks Books And Stuff** for helping spread the word. Keep doing what you're doing. Your shows are great, and they help so much.

Huge thanks to **Sadie Hartmann** and **Night Worms** for the brilliant cover reveal. The work you do is out of kindness and love for the horror community, and it's a beautiful thing.

Thank you to **Black Quill Editing** for catching what I missed and making this book fundamentally better.

Finally, we come to the two people I am grateful to first and foremost.

My mom, **Cindy Applegate**, has never in her life failed to support me, no matter what I was trying to do. She celebrates every stride I make like I just scored the winning touchdown at the Super Bowl. I get my love of horror, my love of reading, and just about everything else from her. Thank you, mom, for doing a terrible job of hiding your Stephen King books, and for letting me watch some genuinely horrific movies when I was a kid. And most of all, thank you for never saying no to buying me a book, even when we were dirt poor and it would have been better to keep the money. For what it's worth, this book (and anything else I write) could never have happened without you.

And finally, my wife, **Stacey Applegate**. My best friend. My instinct was to write about how selfless she is, how she works so hard, how grateful I am to her for the ways she improves the lives of myself and our daughters, how she treats my writing like it matters—and all those things are true. But it's a disservice. Instead I want to tell you about her, because I want you to love her as much as I do for who she is, not for how she relates to me.

She is funny. She makes me laugh every day. She is insanely smart. She's a lifelong TV and movie fan, and there's nobody better to pick apart a movie with. She loves Jane Austen, zombie movies, and she's discovering Shirley Jackson. She loves to research, learn, and share. She's so fun to talk to and to listen to. When she explains the plot of a movie, she explains the *whole* plot of the movie. When someone near her is upset or in trouble, she can't stop trying to help. She is so full of love, not only for our family but for every human being she meets. She gives people the benefit of the doubt. She is conscientious. She cares so much about so many things. Sometimes she forgets to take care of herself, and I wish she would stop that. She's a thoughtful mom and wife. She works too hard. She drives others to be better. She sees the good in (almost) everyone. She constantly works to be the change she wants to see in the world. God, I hope I've done her any kind of justice. Stacey, thank you for being who you are. I am in awe of you, and I always will be.

All of you mean the world to me. I hope you know that.

OTHER WORKS YOU SHOULD READ

Since this is my first and only book, I thought I'd use the opportunity to call out some excellent works by some of the people who have supported, encouraged, and helped me along the way. The list is long, so get to reading!

...and this isn't all! If you're unfamiliar with any of the authors below, I'd suggest you follow all these great people on your platform of choice, and get ready to be introduced to the wide world of indie dark/weird/fantasy/horror fiction. Buckle up!

By Elford Alley

Find Us

The Last Night In The Damned House

Ash and Bone

In Search Of The Nobility, TX Wildman

We Will Find A Place For You

By Cassandra Yorke

Mary, Everything

By Alexis DuBon

"Bug Bite" in Field Notes From A Nightmare from Dread Stone Press

"Just Another Cautionary Tale" on the Wicked Library (podcast)

Multiple entries in the Hundred Word Horror anthology series from Ghost Orchid Press

By Gordon B. White

As Summer's Mask Slips and Other Disruptions

Rookfield

By Red Lagoe

Lucid Screams

Dismal Dreams

By Joshua Marsella

Scratches

Severed

Hunger For Death

By Eric Raglin

Nightmare Yearnings

Extinction Hymns (coming soon)

By Alex Ebenstein

Field Notes From A Nightmare (Editor)

Dose of Dread (editor, web series from Dread Stone Press)

"Glowing Eyes" in The Cryptid Chronicles, February 2021

"Ghost Vision" in Trembling With Fear, January 2021

"My Brother's Keeper" in Boneyard Soup Magazine, January 2021

By Patrick Barb

"The Great Angel Deluge and How It (Nearly) Ruined My Special Day"
in Tales to Terrify podcast, October 2021

"My Dad the Monster King" in Boneyard Soup Magazine, October 2021

"The Other Half of the Battle," Tales to Terrify podcast, September
2021

"The Crack in the Ceiling" in Dose of Dread, Dread Stone Press,
June 2021

By Rena Mason

The Evolutionist

East End Girls

By Steve Clark

The Collapse of Ordinary

Brandon Applegate lives and writes in a parched suburban hell-scape near Austin, Texas with his wife and two daughters who have so far failed to eat him. He spends his free time finding creative ways to deal with his Chupacabra infestation.

For more visit bapplegate.com.

twitter.com/brandonappleg8

goodreads.com/brandonapplegate

amazon.com/author/brandonapplegate